I'M GLAD I FOUND YOU THIS CHRISTMAS

CP WARD

AMMFA
PUBLISHING

1

LAST CHANCE SALOON

WOULD HE PICK UP THIS TIME?

Maggie stared at Dirk's picture on her smartphone's screen, waiting for the inevitable referral to voicemail. What had happened to him recently? She knew he was busy at the company—and being the youngest member of the board of directors in the company's history made it no surprise—but recently she'd begun to feel … well, she knew what Renee would say. Needing the comfort of her best friend's words, she hung up and rang Renee instead.

Like clockwork, Renee answered on the second ring.

'Lo?'

'Ren, it's me.'

'Mag? A bit early for lonely hearts. What's up? You got an hour for coffee?'

Maggie leaned over her shoulder, glancing up at the work schedule taped next to the clock. At the same time she noticed she only had six minutes left on her break.

Her shift manager, Dolores "Thundercloud" Smith, would come deluging down on her freedom if she caught Maggie on the phone.

'Look, I can't really talk now, but it's about Dirk.'

'Of course it is. What else would it be?'

'He's not answering his phone.'

'That's probably because he's womanizing. You know what I think of him. Dirk the—'

'That was a once-off. He promised me it wouldn't happen again. It's just that since his promotion he's been absent more than he's been around. This time last year we were planning to move in together, but now it's just work, work, work—'

'I'll be waiting outside yours with a bottle of red at six-fifteen. On second thoughts, screw it. Make it six-ten. We'll get sloshed and go over everything that's happened since we last got together.'

'Renee, I couldn't put it on you again—'

'He needs a slapdown if you ask me. I mean, come on, Maggie. Have you looked in the mirror recently? You're gorgeous.'

Maggie felt her cheeks flush. 'You're just trying to cheer me up—'

'Break's over, Coates!'

Maggie scowled. She hadn't noticed the dimming of the atmosphere with the onset of rain. 'Gotta go,' she said. 'It's about to chuck down in here.'

'Six-oh-five!'

'Right!'

The door swung open, and a black-clad monster squeezed through. Dolores Smith glared at Maggie with eyes that were too large for a face that sloped backward into her hair, eyes that were perhaps too heavy, and the reason why her head seemed to have sunk into her body, leaving no trace of neck.

'Get back on the floor, Coates,' the Thundercloud snapped. 'Do I look like a charity?'

'No, Ms. Smith,' Maggie said, slipping her phone back into her bag, which she pressed into a locker, closed the door and swiftly turned a key.

'You're two minutes over break. I expect to see you still folding shirts at two minutes past six.'

'Of course.'

Dolores lifted a hand and turned it upward with a strangely exaggerated movement. Her thumb poked up. Then, with a sinister grin, she hoicked her thumb back over her shoulder. 'Move.'

True to her word, Renee was waiting outside Maggie's flat when she arrived. Even though Maggie was nearly twenty minutes late, Renee flashed a wide grin and lifted up two carrier bags.

'Wine,' she said. Then, holding up the other, she added, 'And this one's comfort food. Tesco's takeaway korma, caramel popcorn, and I got us *Frozen* on DVD. Girls' night.'

'*Frozen?*'

'It was on special offer. Two for one.'

'Oh. What was the other one?'

'*Dora the Explorer*. It's for my niece.'

Maggie laughed. '*Frozen* it is, then.'

Renee, petite, blonde-bobbed, and stunning in everything she wore, was an almost perfect person—kind to animals and people, a charity donator, an ever-present at fundraisers, and her job as an administrator in a children's care home was almost a cliché—and therefore impossible not to love.

'So, tell me what's going on,' Renee said as Maggie let them into her flat.

'Let me make the tea first.'

When they were settled on the sofa with the curry, tea, and popcorn arranged on the coffee table in front of them, with the *Frozen* DVD looping through its main menu sequence, Maggie finally let out a sigh.

'I was hoping it would be this year,' she said.

'What?'

'That he'd finally … you know. Pop the question.'

'Oh.'

'Four years we've been together, and we still don't even live together. I mean, that was supposed to happen last year, but then he got promoted and had to move to London.'

'You could have moved down there. He did ask, didn't he?'

'Yeah, of course. I mean, I think he mentioned it once. But I can't leave my mother, you know that. Her hip is getting worse and she needs me close by.'

Renee sighed. 'You're in Cambridge and Dirk's down in London. It's not going to work.'

'It's only an hour on the train. A lot of people commute from here. The only reason Dirk won't is because Saunders & Co gave him a flat in Kensington. I know he wants me to move in with him….'

Renee turned on the sofa and put her hands on Maggie's knees. She cocked her head in that puppy dog way, and Maggie knew a home truth was coming.

'It's commitment avoidance. Can't you see that? He might as well have a billboard above his head with "single and loving it" written in gold lettering.'

'You're not being fair—'

'He cheated on you once; he'll do it again. Pass me that naan.'

'Here. He was so sorry. He, um, cried.'

'Oh, there's a surprise. Look. You don't rise to the board of directors at the age of thirty-two—'

'He's thirty-five.'

'—thirty-five without having a few tricks up your sleeve. Honest people don't get rich. Look at you.'

'I'm not honest.'

'Oh, come on, Maggie. You're so pure you bathe in distilled water. And you're so kind that even though your boss treats you like a piece of excrement on a farmer's shoe, you won't quit your job.'

'I like the shop! And the Thundercloud's only there three days a week. June, our scheduler, tries to give everyone a couple of days' break.'

'You're avoiding my point. What I'm trying to say is that Dirk the … whatever … has cooled on you. He's like a calving iceberg. You've been together so long that he's never known anything else. Now he's got a bit of freedom so he's racing away as fast as he can.'

'Right into London's shipping lanes, yeah?'

Renee narrowed her eyes. She was trying to look angry, but she just looked cuter than ever. Maggie wished she could hate the way her best friend did that.

'The female ones for sure. Trust me on this.'

Maggie shook her head. 'No, you're wrong. I know you are.'

'You're just in denial. Come on, let's crack the wine.'

'It's only seven o'clock!'

'So?'

Twenty minutes later, with *Frozen* playing in the background with the sound turned low, and half the wine already drunk, Renee turned to Maggie with that familiar look on her face.

'Okay, I have a plan.'

'No, please. I'm sure your social worker friends are really nice and all, but Dirk's the only one for me.'

'It's about Dirk, you dummy. I've thought of a way to find out for sure if he still likes you.'

'What?'

'A Christmas vacation. Somewhere remote, somewhere romantic.'

'Don't be ridiculous. It's only November.'

'Yeah, and how long has the Thundercloud already been playing your Chrimbo hits CD at work?'

'Actually, we're still on Celine Dion. Christmas is one of her—many—pet hates. She usually caves by December, though. As soon as the trees go up in the storefront she has no more excuse.'

'Anyway. What I have in mind is somewhere the two of you can be alone, all cosy like, where you can find out for sure what Dirk really feels about you. It'll be perfect.

A bit of snow on the ground, a warm fire, a real Christmas tree with presents piled underneath, loads of wine, a double bed—'

'All right, all right. I get your point.'

'It'll be so romantic you'll have honey dripping from the ceiling. He'll have to ask you to marry him for sure.'

'And what if he doesn't?'

Renee shrugged. 'Then you'll know what he really feels, won't you? Nothing ventured, nothing gained, right?'

Maggie sighed. 'I could spend the next hour trying to talk you round, but you're set on this, aren't you? You're not going to shut up about it until I say yes.'

Renee shook her head. 'Nope.'

'Only one question, then. Where? It's got to be cheap, because I'm skint. The Thundercloud halved our Christmas bonuses this year.'

'We'll get hunting as soon as the movie's over. Gosh, Kristoff's such a dish, isn't he?'

2

DECISIONS

Saturday was Maggie's day off. Renee was waiting for her in a Starbucks in Cambridge city centre, an iPad already set up on a stand on the table.

'You're late,' Renee said, her little button nose wearing a touch of red as though it were already winter outside. 'I took the liberty of ordering you a Caramel Mousse Frappuccino and a butternut donut.'

'Sounds like a heart attack on a plate.'

'You'll have one when you look at some of these places. They're just magnificent.'

Maggie slid into a chair as the waitress arrived, unloading Renee's excessive order onto the table. A tingle of reluctance was nagging her, as though aware that Renee, in all her perfectness, had got carried away with everything. However, Maggie had checked the Christmas roster and it was her turn to have Christmas week off this year, having worked right up to Christmas Eve last year, plus the sales days from Boxing Day to

New Year—Dirk had gone on a business trip with some associates to Malaga—so she was free to go on vacation should she find somewhere suitable, but there were other things to consider. One of them was cost.

'Canada,' Renee said with an excessive intake of breath, as though stepping out on to a mountaintop at the end of a long hike. 'Wiltonsville, a little hamlet north of Whistler. Look at these cabins. They're only accessible by snowmobile, so you're totally cut off from civilization. Imagine waking up to these vistas.'

Maggie frowned. 'Eighty dollars a night, not including flights and transfers. I can barely afford the train fare to the airport.'

Renee grimaced. 'Don't give up; we're just getting started. Next one—what about Lapland? Santa's home —where could be better? Look at these glass igloos. You could lie on your back with Dirk while watching the Northern Lights through the roof.'

Maggie rolled her eyes then pointed at the screen. 'Look at these reviews. Half of them say it snowed and they didn't see anything. And these prices? Sure, it's cheap in November, but over Christmas it's nearly double the price.'

Renee tapped her nose. 'This isn't looking promising, is it? Why can't you just get Dirk to pay?'

'It's hardly romantic if I book a special getaway then ask him for his credit card number, is it?'

'You'll find out if he truly loves you. Plus, he's loaded, isn't he? Eighty grand a year?'

Maggie shrugged. 'A little more. Plus bonuses. Slightly better than nine-fifty an hour, but it's not about the money, is it? We were together when he was just working at his father's company for minimum wage. I'm paying for this trip, and that's the end of it. Keep looking.'

'There's nothing good on Trip Advisor or Yahoo. Just a few slums. Didn't realise you could do Christmas breaks in Romania or Lithuania. Wouldn't fancy it much myself, but each to their own.'

'Let me have a look. Let's just Google it and see what comes up.'

As Maggie reached for the tablet, Renee shook her head. 'No, girl, no. You're not thinking enough outside the box. You think you'll find that special place in a conventional way?'

Renee ran her fingers over the screen and an old search engine Maggie remembered from her pre-university days appeared.

'Where'd you find that? Can it even cope with the full alphabet?'

Renee winked. 'Let's find out.' She typed in "Romantic Christmas getaway location ideal for getting a marriage proposal but off the beaten path and cheap" and clicked enter. A searching icon appeared.

'I think you're pushing it,' Maggie said. 'I guess we could just go to Centre Parcs. I heard they have some fun package deals. The Thundercloud goes every year.'

'You really think you'll be in the spirit for getting hitched while lying in the Thundercloud's bed?'

'Well, I doubt we'd get the exact same room….'

'But just the thought of it? Come on, have faith, Mag.'

'I haven't had that in a long time.'

'I've noticed. Aha! Look at this.'

A website had appeared on the screen. Even from the header it looked either a remnant from 1995 or a scam. "PERFECT WINTER HOLIDAYS WITHOUT LEAVING THE UK." Then, the small print: "Hollydell is a unique Christmas village in the Scottish highlands. Perfect for that quiet Christmas getaway with your loved ones. Snow guaranteed."

Renee puffed out her cheeks into two perfect circles. 'And there we have it.'

'There aren't any pictures!'

'Well, it's an old website, isn't it? But look, they're still taking bookings. And those prices … wow. It's a complete bargain.'

Maggie shook her head. '"Snow guaranteed." What do they do, sprinkle a bit of flour on the trees? It's Scotland. They don't get any snow, do they?'

'They get a bit. I heard there are a couple of ski resorts up there. Come on, Mags. And look at these reviews! "Perfect." "Idyllic." "Breath-taking."'

'They're all just one word. That's totally fake. I'll show up and it'll be a dirty business hotel in the middle of nowhere. It'll probably be abandoned, just me and some crusty old caretaker. I have such a bad feeling about this.'

Renee smiled. She tucked a lock of hair behind her ear, reminding Maggie how remarkably elf-like Renee's ears were. They really did have that little point that could have got her a bit part in *Lord of the Rings*.

'I'm your BFF,' Renee said. 'Just trust me. There's

something about this place that just clicks. I mean, it's got "holly" in the title. And a dell, that's like a quaint valley or something, right?'

'It's also a laptop.'

'You're so sceptical. Look, how about this? If it sucks, I'll buy the coffees for a whole year. Deal?'

Renee held up one hand and hooked her little finger. The coffee shop lights glittered off perfectly manicured fingernails with little dabs of red like a robin's breast.

With a sigh, Maggie lifted her hand and gave Renee's pinkie a little tug with her own. 'Throw in the donuts and you're on.'

'Gotcha. Let's book it.'

3

INVITATIONS AND PREPARATIONS

DIRK'S PICTURE CONTINUED TO FLASH. MAGGIE WAS just about to give up, when a timer appeared, and Dirk's voice said, 'Yeah?'

Maggie felt a tingle both of excitement and worry. What if he said no? What if he had to fly off to Malaga again this year?

'Hey, Dirk.'

'Hey, Pretty Pea. What's up?'

Maggie felt an immediate tingle of anger. It was a new nickname, one which made him sound like her dad. She'd told him she didn't like it, but that had only made him use it more often.

'Dirk ... I ... are you still coming back to Cambridge this weekend?'

'Yeah, about that. I'm sorry, Pretty Pea, but it looks like I've got to work. It's just this new job; I have to put the hours in during my first year, you know. The flat's looking good. You should come down sometime and check it out.'

The vagueness of "sometime" was another of what Renee would call a red flag marker. Apparently, Dirk's speech and voicemails were littered with them.

'Not to worry,' Renee had told her last time they had met. 'Your cottage is booked for two. If he doesn't show I'd be happy to fill in.'

'I'd love to,' Maggie said. 'I've got to work this weekend, but next is free—'

Dirk laughed. Maggie was tempted to click the icon for video call, but she was afraid of the look in his eyes. What if he was distracted, or appeared bored? What if he was out with someone else?

'Next weekend I have a conference,' Dirk said. 'We're as busy as each other, aren't we? Don't worry, Pretty Pea, we'll see each other over Christmas.'

Maggie felt as though a train had hit her right in the heart. Christmas was still five weeks away. She'd hoped to see him in person at least a couple of times before that.

'About Christmas … there's something I've been wanting to tell you.'

'Oh yeah? Are you working? That's a shame, but I guess if you are it can't be helped. There's a trip a couple of the guys are planning that I guess I could join if you're not free. Nothing special, just a bit of a management team-builder out to Portugal.'

Maggie sagged in her chair. He didn't want to be with her. She could hear it in his voice. She was thinking to give him some vague excuse to end the call, but then

Renee's voice, endlessly positive, chirped up in her mind: 'Just tell him!'

'I booked somewhere for us,' she blurted, immediately covering her mouth, worried that he'd take it as shouting. 'It's a Christmas getaway. I took a week off from the twentieth. I thought we could go up there together.'

'Oh really?' A hint of amusement in his voice. 'Where is it? Canada?'

Maggie inwardly scowled. 'Scotland. A place called Hollydell. It's described in the brochure as a perfect Christmas village.'

'Nice. What's it look like in the pictures?'

Maggie hesitated. 'Um, it looks, er, romantic.'

Dirk's laugh bordered on condescending. 'Ha, we're never going to weed that out of you, are we?'

Maggie opened her mouth to reply, but felt an overwhelming urge to cry. 'I thought it would be nice,' she croaked, holding back tears. 'I thought we could spend Christmas together, just the two of us.'

She heard him sigh. Then, to her surprise, he said, 'Sure. I'll be there.'

'You can make it? Really?'

'Well, I can't make the twentieth. So sorry. I have a big meeting in London that I have to attend. But I can come by the twenty-first or second. I tell you what—you go up first and get settled in, and I'll follow you up a day or so later. I'll bring a special surprise, something to really cheer you up.'

Maggie frowned before twigging what he meant. Huh. Really? Could it be the ring she had been dreaming of? She needed to end this call RIGHT NOW and call Renee. Oh God. Her perfect friend was right, and they hadn't even got there yet. He was going to ask. He was going to ASK.

'That sounds nice,' she squeaked, barely able to lift he voice above a whisper. 'I'll message you with the directions. You can't drive, apparently. There's a special train.'

Dirk groaned. 'You can drive anywhere. But if it'll make you happy, I'll go mass transit with the rest of the herd. I'll wear extra aftershave to compensate.'

Berating the poor was another of Renee's red flags —since, technically, both Maggie and Renee were minimum wage workers—but Maggie ignored it. 'I can't wait,' she gasped, perhaps with a little too much eagerness. 'It's going to be the perfect holiday.'

'Sure, Pretty Pea. Sure it will.'

After hanging up, Maggie rushed to call Renee. Her friend answered briefly to say she was stuck at traffic lights on her way to spend an afternoon playing board games with a disabled lady, but that she'd call back later. Hanging up, Maggie ran in little circles, wishing there was someone else she could call. Her mum would be at work—but she wasn't too hot on Dirk since his move to London—and none of her other friends would want to know. Instead, she did the only other thing she could think of to settle her nerves.

She went shopping.

Christmas was still a long way off, but she managed to pick up a nice pair of snow boots and a jacket with a fake fur trim which would look nice in the snow days.

Walking out of the shop into a warm, sunny afternoon, however, she had a crisis of confidence. It hadn't snowed in Cambridge over Christmas since she had been a little girl. Sure, Scotland was way farther north, but was it really going to be much different? She'd been watching the weather forecast with interest, and it was still practically beach weather all over the U.K. What was the likelihood that their remote, romantic getaway was a windy shack on a hill somewhere, battered constantly by the driving rain? Images of power cuts and doors that got stuck in the damp and baths with cracks and spiders and weird locals peering in through the windows and—

'Stop!'

She shouted so loud at herself that an old lady walking past gave her a bemused glance. Maggie smiled, muttered sorry under her breath, and then did that terribly British thing of talking to herself in quiet tones as though to soften the blow of her sudden outburst. She was working herself up into a panic, she knew it. What happened to being all girl power and feminist and—

Deep breath. He'll be there. It'll all be fine.

And it'll definitely snow.

4

DEPARTURE

'SO, YOU'RE ALL SET. YOU'VE GOT YOUR PASSPORT, right?'

'My … I don't … what?'

Renee giggled and patted Maggie on the arm. 'I'm having a laugh. No, you don't need it. Except maybe to check in. But they're hardly going to turn you away after travelling from Cambridge, are they? You've got your driver's license?'

Maggie took a deep breath. 'Yeah, I've got it.'

'And you've got enough underwear, just in case there's no washing machine?'

'What? You never said—'

'Relax!'

Maggie tried to calm herself, but was aware she was starting to panic. 'It's not too late, you know. I can pull the whole trip. I haven't paid anything upfront. I mean, Dirk might not even show up. We can have a girls'

Christmas. Drink some wine, watch, um, *Frozen* again….'

Renee gave her a comforting pat on the arm. 'It'll all be fine. Just trust Auntie Renee. Tell me again about the journey. It sounds so romantic.'

Maggie had read over the printout from the web page so many times she could recite it with barely a mistake. '"Catch the 7.15 a.m. train to Edinburgh Waverley. From there, take the 1.03 to Inverness. At Inverness, find Platform 7A and wait for the 4.31 on the Hollydell Line. There is only one train per day—don't miss it. The train is a single carriage and stops only once, at Hollydell Firth at exactly 5 p.m. Do not be alarmed when you exit the station. To reach Hollydell, walk up the road through the trees for approximately three hundred metres. The village will appear in front of you. The village hall is on your left. Someone will be waiting to show you to your cottage."'

Renee hummed, her hands pressed together under her chin. '"The village will appear in front of you." Sounds like it's magic, doesn't it?'

Maggie resisted the urge to say something negative. 'Assuming it's even there. I tried to find it on Google Maps, but it's a black spot. That could mean anything. Perhaps I'm walking into a military alien abduction facility.'

'Well, at least Dirk's coming to meet you. He can be your knight in shining armour to save you from all those pesky E.T.s.'

'Yeah, sure.'

Renee was still beaming and staring off into space as a loudspeaker announced the approach of a train.

'Well, here goes.'

Renee pulled Maggie into a bear hug. She smelled faintly of Yves Saint Laurent and Starbucks Latte. No doubt Maggie smelled of fear, but she forced herself to take a deep breath.

'It'll be fine,' Renee said. 'Haven't I told you to trust me?'

'Several times.'

'And if you get phone reception, be sure to give me a call to let me know how it is. Send me some pics. I'm having Christmas lunch down at the children's home this year. A few pics of your special moment'll cheer them up.'

The train pulled in. Guards opened the doors and a stream of passengers climbed down, bustling along the platform.

'Right, here goes.'

'And remember, I'll see you on the twenty-seventh. We've got our lunch date, so don't forget. I want to see your new ring. Gosh, it should be massive, what with Dirk's salary.'

'I won't forget.'

'Unless the two of you decide to extend your stay over New Year,' Renee added. 'I'd forgive that, but anything else … nope.'

'Ren, I've got to go. Thanks for everything.'

Maggie lifted her case and climbed onto the train. Renee waved at her from the platform.

'Good luck, Mags! Break a leg! Or don't, as the case may be!'

As the train started to pull away, Renee tucked her hair behind her ear, and Maggie saw that little point again. Perhaps her friend was magical after all. She could only hope so. It might need magic to save her relationship with Dirk.

5

THE JOURNEY NORTH

THE CAMBRIDGE-TO-EDINBURGH TRAIN WASN'T BUSY, but each time it stopped and groups of families climbed on board, off on some adventure, or a returning relative climbed down into the arms of their waiting loved ones, Maggie was reminded that she was on her way to what she hoped would be a romantic holiday retreat on her own. For perhaps the fiftieth time, she opened her phone and checked for messages, but there was only the same message Dirk had sent her yesterday: *I'll be there. Don't worry. Xx*

There were only two kisses instead of the usual three. Had he been in a hurry, or was she just paranoid? The temptation to call Renee for her opinion was overwhelming, but she'd only been on the train an hour and Renee was possibly still driving home.

'Get a grip on yourself,' she muttered, picking up the can of wine she had bought last night and stuffed into her bag as a safety precaution in case the shop at

Cambridge station wasn't yet open. It hadn't been, and there would be no buffet car until she changed at Peterborough in another half an hour. She hadn't opened the can yet, but it was so, so tempting.

As a large, white-bearded man eased past her down the aisle, holding a polystyrene cup of coffee from the vending machine at the station, Maggie slipped the wine back into her bag. She must look like a proper lush. She was just so terrified of something going wrong, despite Renee's assurances. She hadn't seen a single picture of Hollydell. It was somewhere deep in the Cairngorms National Park, but it wasn't showing up on Google Maps and the only pictures she had of the area showed barren, exposed hills.

It was a scam, it had to be.

She nearly stayed on the train when it got to Peterborough, waiting for it to begin the return journey to Cambridge. Only when a disgruntled cleaner shambled through and waved her off the train did she climb down on to a now empty platform. Perhaps if she left her bag behind on purpose? She'd have to stay. She hadn't paid for anything yet except her train ticket, and she could put Dirk off with a quick message. He'd probably be pleased.

A loudspeaker announced the arrival of the Edinburgh train. To Maggie's frustration, it was on the opposite platform, meaning she had no choice but to board it or look like a plonker who'd gone to the wrong platform by mistake.

At least she had a comfortable seat facing forward. She put her bag in the overhead rack then kicked off her shoes. Someone had left a novel in the pocket of the seat in front. Maggie pulled it out, but *Hearts Torn Asunder: Fifteen Tales of Loneliness* didn't really appeal, so she tossed it onto the seat across the aisle and instead took out a newspaper she had bought in Cambridge.

The front page had a picture of a motorway pileup. The second page had an article about an ongoing stock market crash, and the third a story about a famous TV star who was caught having an affair with a co-star.

With a grimace, Maggie reached into her bag and took out the can of wine. Perhaps it was time to open it after all.

A new message blinked on her phone. She opened it, hoping it was Dirk, but it was only Renee, checking in: *Did you make your connection? Remember who's buying next year's coffees if you chicken out.*

Yeah, I made it, Maggie messaged back. *Having a great time.*

What did I tell you? Of course you are, Renee replied almost immediately, as usual shocking Maggie with the speed of her reply, as though she'd been waiting all morning for a message. *Got to go to work now. Check in when you get there!*

Maggie actually managed to doze much of the way to Edinburgh, the stress perhaps making her sleepy, but after she made her connection to Inverness, the nerves started to kick in, and she found herself leaning forward in her seat, peering out of the window as though every house the train passed could be her holiday retreat.

Nice one … what a dump … too old … flats?

Be brave, Renee messaged her just as the train was

pulling into Inverness, as though aware how Maggie was feeling. Dirk, for his part, hadn't messaged her at all.

Inverness's train station was a lot smaller than Maggie had expected, and the only signs to anything other than the city centre were to a shuttle bus heading for Loch Ness. She looked around for platform 7A, but couldn't see it anywhere. Platform 7 just ended, there was no 7A on the map, and no signs pointing to it. She took a toilet stop, briefly messaged Renee to say the whole thing looked like a scam, then went to the ticket office just to confirm what she thought before buying a ticket back to Cambridge.

The lady in the ticket office had rosy cheeks as though she drank too much port, and was wearing a Christmas hat with a flashing red light on the top.

'How can I help you?' she said with a welcoming smile.

Maggie felt her cheeks turning as red as the hat's light. 'Well, this is going to sound stupid, like I'm Harry Potter or something, but I'm looking for a platform called 7A. There isn't one, is there? I mean, I booked online, and you can never really trust the internet, can you, not even these days. I mean there are more fake sites than real ones. I should have been more careful—'

'Through that door,' the lady said, pointing. 'Renovations a couple of years ago left it a little cut off from the rest of the station, and there's only the one daily train after all. Not our busiest line, for sure. Oh, look at that.'

'What?'

The lady was looking past Maggie's shoulder.

Maggie turned, her jaw dropping open in surprise.

Through the station's doors she saw snow falling in the courtyard outside.

'Been years since we've had a white Christmas,' the lady said. 'Perhaps you've brought us good luck. You'd better hurry if you're going to catch your train. It's leaving in two minutes. Just follow the gravel path through the bushes.'

Maggie nodded thanks, grabbed her bag and pushed through the door. She found herself on a pretty path lined by flowerbeds. A grass bank on one side led up to the station's mainline, but the path meandered through a garden of little conifers, some of which had been decorated with Christmas lights.

The platform was out of sight around a side building, so Maggie picked up her case and ran, the wheels ineffective on the gravel. As she came around the corner she saw the train sitting at the platform.

'Huh.'

She stopped dead, staring at the column of smoke rising out of a chimney near the train's front. It was a tiny steam engine pulling a single carriage wide enough only for a line of seats against the window. The train was black, but its wheel rims and arches were painted red. As she approached she could tell from the creak and groan of the wheels that it was very old, but someone obviously loved it enough to look after it.

It let out a belch of steam with a long hiss. A horn gave a single toot, then the driver climbed down and walked along the length of the train, opening the doors as he went.

A rotund man with a thick beard and a slight potbelly, the driver tipped his hat to Maggie then waved to one of the doors. A ticker sign over the door clicked over from INVERNESS to HOLLYDELL.

'All aboard for Hollydell,' he said. 'Would you like help with your case?'

'No, thank you … oh, sure. That's very kind.'

The man smiled as he lifted Maggie's case, then stepped back to allow her onto the train. He passed the case up then shut the door.

Maggie had her choice of seats, so she took one up front, just behind the quaint locomotive, through which the nostalgic smell of coal and steam wafted like a welcome roast dinner. She had thought she disliked steam trains, having been taken on one by her grandparents many years ago that had a leaky roof and a broken window which meant they were choking on steam and smoke the whole way, but sitting here now, she realised she liked it. There was something warm and comforting about the little toot of the horn, the chug-chug as the wheels started to move, the hiss of steam as it squeezed through the boiler pipes.

Through a window into the locomotive, she watched the driver shovel a few spadefuls of coal into the boiler then take his seat. The horn tooted, and they were off.

Inverness fell away behind them as the Hollydell train cut through the town, following a meandering route that took them through quiet suburbs along a line designed both for calm and discretion. Trees grew in ordered rows on either side, and the few people Maggie saw lifted their hands to wave with smiles on their faces.

Soon Inverness was behind them, and they sped through pastureland and rolling fields, between moorland valleys and around the edges of rippling lochs. Maggie, who at first had watched with interest at the countryside as they passed, a light dusting of snow beginning to cover everything, found herself getting sleepy.

So far so good, she messaged Renee. *It's even snowing. Not quite sure how romantic this village is going to be, but at least it seems to exist.*

I told you, didn't I? came the reply. *Trust Auntie Renee. I always know best.*

In the distance, the hills turned into snow-capped mountains. Even though the carriage was warm, it looked quite chilly outside, so Maggie pulled a sweater out of her bag and slipped it over her head. Leaning against the window, she tried not to close her eyes.

She must have dozed off, because the next thing she knew, they were passing through a forested ravine, several centimetres of fresh snow lying beneath the trees. Evening had come on, and the only light came from inside the carriage and the occasional glimpse of a purple sky.

Maggie sat up, alarmed that she had fallen asleep. She checked the time on her phone and found she'd been asleep nearly twenty minutes. She glanced at the driver, who still had his back to her, his concentration on the line ahead. Where were they? They could be anywhere by now.

The horn tooted, and the train began to slow. Up ahead, the line made a gentle arc through tall pines, and then Maggie saw it: a quaint stonewalled train station, its lights a welcoming orange, and a sign lit up by Christmas lights which read:

WELCOME TO HOLLYDELL
ENJOY YOUR STAY

The train pulled in, touching lightly against a set of buffers. So, this really was the end of the line. The driver stood up then opened a window in the back of the cab. The smell of coal wafted in.

'Everybody off,' he called with a cheerful grin.

Maggie pulled on her jacket and checked she had everything with her, but by the time she had reached the doors the driver had pulled them open. He took her case then offered her a hand to help her down.

'Welcome to Hollydell. Miss Maggie Coates, isn't it?'

Maggie was a little taken aback. 'How did you know?'

The driver smiled. 'We're not exactly overrun with visitors, as you can see. Hollydell is a place only for special people. I'd like to extend my warmest welcome. My name is Andrew. I drive the train, deliver the mail, and do a few other odd jobs around the village. Now, we're a little bit farther down the valley here, so to get to the town proper, just take the road opposite. The lights will be on by now, so don't worry about getting lost. It's not far. The first building you'll see is the village hall.

Go in there and someone will show you to your cottage.'

He reached out a hand. Maggie smiled and shook it. It was warm and soft, and for some reason reminded her of a comforting log fire.

'I'm sure I'll see you around,' he said. 'Don't miss the Christmas Eve extravaganza in the village square. It's an open air event and it's a lot of fun. Then we have the theatre on the twenty-third … but anyway, you'll find out more when you get to the village. Enjoy your stay.'

He climbed back onto the train, leaving Maggie alone on the platform. She pulled out her phone, found she had one bar of reception, and fired off a quick message to Renee.

Made it!

Then, picking up her bag, she headed for the exit.

No one was waiting at the ticket entrance, so Maggie walked right through. She found herself facing a small square with a raised flowerbed in the centre, on which stood a beautiful Christmas tree, its lights glittering. Everything was dusted by a few centimetres of snow, but it wasn't overly cold, perhaps only a couple of degrees below zero, just low enough to stop the snow from spoiling. Maggie let out a long sigh. If only Renee could see this—

Dirk. What about Dirk?

She realised she had barely thought about him since leaving Inverness. She felt a pang of guilt, realising that part of her now hoped he wouldn't show up. This was her trip, her holiday, and Dirk's intrusion with his flippancies and lack of consideration for her feelings didn't feel welcome.

She frowned. This was the man she wanted to marry whom she was thinking about with so much negativity. She shook her head. Perhaps she'd just been a little on edge recently, and the shock of finding that Hollydell actually existed was playing havoc with her feelings. She would surely settle once she'd found her cottage.

Overhead, the sky had cleared, and a field of stars shone above steep forested hills. To her left the valley opened up, revealing the distant rises of mountains. And now, as her eyes adjusted, she saw that just past where the train line ended was a small lake, its surface partly iced over.

Was she really still in Scotland? It didn't feel right. The hills were too steep, there were too many trees, too much snow. She felt like she'd gone through a time warp into some mythical new land.

She stepped out into the road. There were no tyre tracks in the snow, only a few carved lines as though someone had come through on giant skis. Then there were the scores of animal prints scattered all over the place.

A tingle of unease trickled down her back. There was a road, for sure, leading into the forest on the other side of the large Christmas tree, but she couldn't see the village yet. What village in this day and age didn't have any cars? What was she likely to find, an actual village or some rundown backwater intent on taking the last of her money?

She took deep breath. Only one way to find out.

6

HOLLYDELL

THE TALL PINES, SOME HUNG WITH STRINGS OF Christmas lights, were a polite distance back from the road to allay any fears of wolves or bears, just in case she wasn't still in Scotland after all, but during her little doze the train had somehow flown all the way to Switzerland or Canada and deposited her somewhere with lots of extra dangers to worry about. The road curved through the trees, refusing to let her see too far ahead, but while there were no signs of cars, someone had at least cleared a line through the snow on the pavement to allow the wheels of her little bag to move freely. She was glad now that she had brought her new boots and jacket, because among the trees the temperature was a couple of degrees cooler than out in the open.

She was starting to wonder if the curving road wasn't some sort of elaborate joke, winding back to the train station where Andrew would be waiting to take her back to Inverness with a mocking grin on his face, when it suddenly opened out, revealing the village up ahead.

Maggie let out a little gasp. Her first instinct was to call Renee, but the thought of intruding on this quaint little place with something as modern as a phone felt wrong. She dropped her hands by her sides, and stared in wonder.

Christmas card perfect, Hollydell spread out before her in a glittering field of Christmas lights. The village hall was a Tudor-style two-storey building just in front of her, then off to the right was a wide square with a Christmas tree standing in its centre, at least three times the height of the one outside the station. A cluster of wooden market stalls stood along one edge of the square, closed up for the night. There was a little post office, and a cluster of restaurants with lights in their windows and the shadows of people inside pressing against the frosted glass. And set back from the village square along roads that wound back into the trees were rows of quaint cottages, their pixie-house pointed roofs laden with snow. Christmas lights lined windows and guttering and garden walls. Snowmen stood on pavements, and sleds stood leaned up against fences. Over the top of everything came the faint tinkle of traditional Christmas music.

'Maggie Coates?' came a woman's voice.

Maggie turned. A woman wearing a woollen check coat was standing outside the village hall's door, beckoning to her.

'Welcome, welcome,' she said, as Maggie walked

over. 'Please come inside. I just made some hot chocolate.'

Maggie couldn't help but smile. As she followed the woman through the door, she slipped her phone out of her pocket, wanting to give Renee a quick message, but she had no bars of reception. With a frustrated frown, she put it back into her pocket.

'Firstly, thank you for coming to Hollydell,' the woman said. 'My name is Ellie. I run things around here, keep everything shipshape. We don't get many visitors these days, but that's intentional. We like to keep Hollydell special for those people who need it most.' She looked up and met Maggie's eyes. 'You see, those who really need us will always find us.'

'I was worried you wouldn't be open,' Maggie said.

'Oh, no worries there. It's scripted that way. Hollydell looks best under lights, as most places do. Hence the late arrival of the train, after sunset. It gives you just enough time to check into your cottage then come back down to the village to get something to eat. Mind you, Hollydell still looks pretty nice during day. I'm sure you'll be very happy here. You're staying until the twenty-seventh, isn't that right?'

'I'm leaving in the morning, yes.'

'Well, feel free to extend your stay. Lots of people do. We only make one booking per cottage per year, just in case.'

Maggie didn't bother to ask how on earth they made any money. She didn't want to spoil the magic with the kind of conversation she might have shared with Renee over a latte after work.

'You like marshmallows and cream or just marshmallows? I know some people like to watch their waistline.'

'Oh.' Maggie smiled. 'Sure, why not? I'm on holiday.'

'That's the spirit. I'll add a chocolate flake while we're at it. You can walk it off in the morning with a stroll around the reindeer farm.'

Maggie stared. 'The what?'

'The reindeer farm. The only one in Scotland. I told you that Hollydell was special.'

'So, we're still in Scotland, then?' Somehow, the revelation was a bit of a let-down, even though she could hardly be anywhere else.

'Of course. Where else would we be?' Ellie lowered her voice. 'But we're in a very special part. There's nowhere quite like Hollydell. Not in Scotland. Not in the world, really. And it's not just the reindeer farm, but everything. Hollydell is like a special Christmas package, waiting to be unwrapped.'

'I'm starting to realise that.'

Ellie smiled, and Maggie smiled back. It seemed that everyone here had the ability to inject a little warmth into her heart. She wondered how Dirk would find it.

Dirk.

Again that pang of guilt that he had slipped so far from her mind. She gave a little shake of her head. She was being silly. He'd be here before she knew it, they'd be together, and everything would work out as it should. Perhaps he'd even bring the ring as she hoped. The last few weeks, she had just been paranoid. Of course he had been busy; he was in a new job after all, and a high-powered one at that. What else should she expect? It was selfish of her really to ask him to devote so much time to her. He'd done so well to get on the board of directors at his age, and on top of everything he had to settle in to a new city. Without doubt, it was her who was the problem, not Dirk. She was just being needy, as always.

'Miss Coates? Are you all right?'

Maggie looked up. 'Oh, sorry. I guess I'm just a little tired from the journey.'

'Well, we'll get you up to your cottage right away, and then I'll show you somewhere to eat. We'll dine together tonight, if you'd like. Just to help you settle in.'

'Oh. Don't you have work to do here?'

Ellie shook her head. 'No, no. I was just waiting for you. And now that you're here, we can close up for the night.'

'Oh, well, thanks.'

Maggie drank her hot chocolate while Ellie tidied up. It was delicious, intensely rich, like a melted chocolate gateau. She ought to be careful not to go too crazy on the food, or Dirk would have another reason not to want her—

Stop it, she could almost hear Renee say.

'Are you ready, then?' Ellie said, switching off a light behind the reception desk and coming around. 'I think it's time we got you up to your cottage.'

7

THE COTTAGE

'IT'S A SHORT WALK UP THIS WAY,' ELLIE SAID, TAKING Maggie's bag and refusing any attempt by Maggie to take it back, even though she was at least half Ellie's age. 'It's not much of a hill, but it can be a little slippery, especially in the mornings.'

'I was surprised at all the snow,' Maggie said.

'Oh, we're tucked away in a little hollow here,' Ellie said, giving Maggie a mysterious look. 'We have our own microclimate. Same for the trees. Only natural pine forest in Scotland.'

'Is that so?'

'Well, I'm not sure, but it sounds about right, doesn't it.'

Maggie wasn't sure what to say. She was still unsure whether Hollydell was a dream or just an elaborate theme park. 'I couldn't find it on Google Maps,' she said.

'No road in, that's why. Just the railway. Ah, here we are. Comfort Cottage.'

Maggie looked up. A white picket gate between two stone walls currently piled with snow led down a snowy path to the front door of a pretty stone cottage. A wreath hung on the door and a string of Christmas lights illuminated a wooden deck on which a table and two chairs stood. Front windows either side of the door glowed with light and a wisp of smoke rose from a chimney at one end.

'Is that really its name?'

'Of course it is,' Ellie said. 'I took the liberty of lighting you a fire and turning on the lights. You'll also find a complimentary bottle of wine on the counter in the kitchen.'

'That's lovely, thanks.'

Ellie handed Maggie a set of keys.

'We're all friends here so you don't need to worry about locking up, but if you want to, you've got front door, back door, shed.'

'What's in the shed?'

'All your outdoor stuff. A sledge, snow shoes, a set of cross country skis. And if there's anything else you want, don't hesitate to ask. We'll do everything we can to accommodate you.'

'That's very kind.'

'Why don't you go in and have a look? I don't want to overpower you too much, so I'll let you look around and get settled in on your own. If you want to meet for dinner, I'll be waiting in Barney's Christmas Kitchen, the first restaurant you'll come to if you walk back down to the square. It serves food until eleven p.m. If you're too tired, don't worry, I eat in there most nights and there are always a few friendly faces around. But if you want some company, I'm available.' She reached out and patted Maggie's arm. 'I hope he comes, you know.'

Maggie frowned. 'I'm sorry?'

'Dirk. Your boyfriend. He's due to arrive the day after tomorrow, isn't he? He's booked on the roster.'

'He'll be here.'

'I hope so.'

Maggie wanted to say something else, that Dirk would certainly come, that she would be an engaged woman by this time next week, and engaged to a high-flying City of London company director no less, but hope was all she had right now.

'I hope so too,' she said.

Ellie patted her arm again, gave Maggie a last smile, then headed off down the street. Maggie took a deep breath, then opened the gate and headed up the path, following the faint line of footprints from earlier which had been buried by the snow.

The front door was unlocked. Maggie went into a bright hallway lit by pretty wall lamps. A small Christmas tree sat on a telephone table near the door. Through the open door of a living room to the right came the crackle of a log fire.

With a contented sigh, Maggie pulled off her boots, put her bag behind the door then closed it, shutting out the winter night. As soon as it was closed, she found herself opening it again, and peering back down the hill just to make sure Hollydell was real.

Pushing through the living room door, she found a compact twin sofa and two armchairs in a semicircle around the cracking fire. A hearth mat with a picture of two sleeping cats lay in front of the stone fireplace over a burnt orange carpet. Behind the two-seater sofa was a larger Christmas tree. A single Christmas card stood on a mantel over the fire, its message *Welcome to Comfort Cottage! Thank you for staying!*

Maggie sat down in one of the armchairs and put her legs up on a stool. Her phone didn't have any reception, but she typed out a message to Renee anyway, planning to take a walk down to the station tomorrow or even tonight after dinner, where she could send it.

I'm in my cottage. I can't believe it, it's just perfect. I feel like I stepped into a Christmas card. Something has to go wrong, it just has to.

A modern flat screen TV stood on a table next to the fireplace. Maggie looked through a stack of DVDs next to it and found almost every seasonal movie she could think of, from *Miracle on 34th Street* and *Home Alone* to *Snoopy's First Christmas*. They had the Christmas theme down so well Maggie found herself wondering what Hollydell did for the rest of the year. Perhaps, like Santa Claus, it just disappeared.

As she leaned back in the armchair, she found she was exhausted, but she hadn't even explored the rest of the house yet, so she made herself get up and go out into the hall. Another door opened onto a neat kitchen-diner with a window out over a back garden which was now shrouded in snow, while a staircase led up to two bedrooms and a small bathroom. Almost as an evolutionary reflex to a past of cheapo, shabby hotels, she tried every light, every tap, switched on and off every appliance, and even tested the windows to make sure they opened and closed.

Everything worked. None of the windows were rusted shut. The water was hot.

It was a true Christmas miracle.

After taking her case upstairs and unpacking her bag into the drawers and cupboards of the bedroom which had been made up, she went back downstairs. The call of a DVD, a hot bath and an early night—perhaps after a sly glass of wine—was almost too much to resist, but her stomach had other ideas.

Time had flown past, and it was nearly eight o'clock already. If she was going to eat, she had to get going, but Ellie had said Barney's Christmas Kitchen served food until eleven p.m. There was still plenty of time for dinner, a nightcap, and to meet a few of the local residents.

With one last longing glance at the comfortable armchair, Maggie pulled on her boots and headed back out into the snow.

8

BARNEY'S CHRISTMAS KITCHEN

A FEW LIGHT CLOUDS HAD COME IN TO OBSCURE THE stars and a gentle, soothing snow was falling. Comfort Cottage was at the end of a row of similar cottages, each set in their own grounds, but beyond it the road headed off into the trees, winding uphill. Ellie had said that there were no roads into or out of the village, so Maggie's curiosity as to where the road went was immediately aroused. With no streetlights that way, it would have to wait until morning.

The cluster of buildings around Hollydell's village square still glittered with lights even at this late hour. As Maggie walked downhill, she spotted Barney's Christmas Kitchen, a discreet sign above the door of a log cabin. The sounds of merriment drifted from inside the frosted windows.

At the door she paused, feeling a momentary nervousness. How would she appear to these people?

Hollydell felt very much like a closed community, and other than herself, Maggie had seen no tourists at all.

'Pull yourself together,' she muttered. 'You don't need Dirk leading you everywhere. You can do this on your own.'

She opened the door. The hum of merriment immediately intensified, surrounding her like a warm blanket. She smiled as she saw Ellie stand up and wave to her from a table across the room. She lifted a hand to wave back, but before she'd taken a single step a waiter had pushed through the tables of laughing, joyful people to lead her through.

'This way, madam,' he said in a slightly Scottish accent. 'Your friends are waiting.'

'My … friends,' she said, wondering if she'd rented a community along with the cottage. Everything ought to feel fake, but it didn't. It felt perfect.

Ellie pulled out a seat for her and practically pushed her into it. Before Maggie could say a word, the older woman had set a plate and cutlery in front of her and was gesturing to a series of bowls and plates.

'We went for the communal feast tonight,' she said. 'Don't worry, you haven't missed anything but a few starters. We've got coronation chicken salad here, cauliflower in olive oil with garlic dip here, potatoes roasted in dark chocolate over here. That's prawn cocktail, and there's some special Hollydell bread. The beef will be here in a moment. No turkey until Christmas, of course.'

'Um, thanks.'

'Just make sure you get up early to walk it all off.

Hollydell is beautiful around sunrise. Don't spend too much time sleeping while you're here. You can do that on the train ride home.'

'Okay, sure.'

Around the table, the other gathered people began to laugh. Ellie waved to each, making introductions. 'This is Sally, who runs the dog sled tours. That's Jim, the town crier—he'll likely wake you up tomorrow. Phillip runs the delicatessen, and Gail over there is one of our catering assistants.'

'Nice to meet you all,' Maggie said, having no time to greet them one by one.

'Oh, and if you have a look back into the kitchens, you'll see Andrew, whom I think you've already met.'

Maggie twisted around. Through a window into the kitchens she saw the train driver, now wearing a cook's whites. He smiled and waved.

'Andrew's my eldest son. You haven't got a nice friend you could invite next year, could you? I'd love to see him finally get married off.'

'A friend? Next year?'

Maggie could barely follow the conversation. Ellie thrust a glass of mulled wine in her hand and raised a toast.

'To our new arrival.'

'Our new arrival!'

They laughed and clinked glasses. In the midst of it all, the waiter put a steaming joint of roast beef down in the middle of the table.

'Wow,' was all Maggie could say.

'Aberdeen Angus,' Ellie said with a hint of pride.

'You'll find a bit of everywhere here in Hollydell, but we know where the best meat comes from, and that's right on our doorstep.'

The others cheered. Maggie heard Renee's voice whispering to her: *Just let your hair down and enjoy it!*

So she did.

~

The time seemed to fly past. Maggie ate too much and drank too much mulled wine. The table was an endless series of cheerful laughter and jokes. No one talked about much other than Christmas and the upcoming events, as though nothing happened in the village at all during the rest of the year.

By the time she stumbled to the door, weary with exhaustion, half of the restaurant had emptied out already, heading back to their cottages to sleep off the food and drink. Christmas music tinkled all around her from speakers hanging from the trees, and a light snow was falling. Maggie stumbled out into the road and peered up, laughing as the snow fell on to her face. She had a vague memory of talking about Dirk to one of the women, about how this was their last chance, that by Boxing Day she would either be engaged or single, but now as she spun around with her arms outstretched, she knew everything would be all right. Dirk would fall in love with Hollydell just as she had, and they would wake up on Christmas morning in each other's arms, more committed than ever.

She looked around at the tinkling of a bell over the

clop of hooves. It must be coming out of the speakers, making her think of Santa Claus –

'Watch out!'

Maggie fell back into a snowdrift just a moment before a small sleigh pulled by a single snorting reindeer came rushing around the corner, skidding past her just inches away from cutting the soles off her shoes. As it veered left, it sprayed her with a curtain of fresh snow.

'Sorry!' came a man's voice as the sleigh rushed off up the road and disappeared around a corner.

'Are you okay?' came Ellie's voice from behind her.

Maggie spat out a mouthful of snow and let Ellie help her up. Her clothes were covered with snow that was slowly melting.

'Um, yeah, I'm sure I'll be fine.'

'So sorry about him. That was Henry, my youngest son. He works on the reindeer farm. He's a bit reckless. This time of year he has to break in the young bucks, so he does it late at night where there aren't many people about. Are you sure he didn't hit you?'

Maggie shook her head. 'No, it's okay. I'm fine.' She stared up the street. The sleigh's tracks glistened in the snow.

Ellie let out an exasperated sigh. 'I'll have a word with him in the morning. He needs to be more careful.'

'It's okay.'

'Well, if you're sure … you get along now. I'll see you around somewhere tomorrow, no doubt. If you have any requests, don't hesitate to come down to the village hall. I'll be on the desk all day.'

As Ellie departed, Maggie started up the hill toward

46

Comfort Cottage. She didn't know whether to feel slighted or bemused by Henry's sudden appearance. In some ways it was nice to get a bit of reality—at least someone was rude here, meaning it couldn't be a magical fantasy land after all. At the same time, there was something fascinating about a man who rode around town at midnight on a mini Santa's sleigh. In Cambridge, Maggie was used to the boy racers revving their souped-up cars around town on a Saturday night, but this was the crazy Hollydell version. Perhaps she'd get to see him around town in the morning, let him apologise face to face.

She thought about walking down to the train station to call Renee (or even Dirk!) but she was exhausted. With a sigh, she headed for Comfort Cottage.

9

HENRY

THE FUG OF A HANGOVER THAT MAGGIE HAD BEEN expecting to wake to wasn't there. As she opened her eyes on December 21st and her first morning in Hollydell, she felt remarkably fresh, as though she'd drunk nothing more than a few glasses of fruit juice. She got up, took a hot, powerful shower, dressed and then went downstairs.

She found the welcome guidebook on the table next to the door where she had left it. Inside were pamphlets advertising everything from evening forest walks to dog sled tours, notifications of a series of Christmas events, and details on the various restaurants and facilities. Maggie felt her cheeks flush at the very thought of an open air Jacuzzi deep in the forest, or a hike up to what was called Santa's Lookout to drink fresh hot chocolate while viewing the Christmas lights of Hollydell from above.

There were a few rules, though. While there were

stacks of DVDs—and more could be borrowed free from the village hall's library—the TV wasn't connected to regular programming. In addition, while the phone in the house could make outgoing calls, there was no Wi-Fi or internet reception in any of the cottages. If you really had to use your mobile phone, a P.S. note read, you could get just enough reception down by the train station, although it advised that for a truly unique experience, you should enjoy being cut off from the rigours of social media for a while.

As soon as she was done reading, Maggie called Renee. Her friend answered on the second ring.

'Maggie? I knew it had to be you. I didn't recognise the number, but I was all ready with the block button in case it was some pervert or a telesales person. How are you doing?'

Maggie sighed. It was great to hear her friend's voice, but it would be even greater if Renee was here with her to experience everything.

'It's like … perfect. I couldn't have dreamt it up. How on Earth they've done it, how it even exists, I can't fathom it. It's perfect down to the last detail. Well, apart from some idiot on a sleigh who sprayed me with snow and stained my new jacket—'

'Santa Claus?'

'Don't be silly. It was a kid. I didn't get a good look at him, but there needed to be some jerk here, just so I didn't get too used to the good stuff.'

'Talking of jerks, has you-know-who arrived yet?'

Maggie smiled. 'You know, I almost forgot. I'm having such a nice time. And he's not a jerk.'

'Did I say that directly? Did I really associate those two words? I think this line's a bit crackly. It's making you hear things.'

'He's due tomorrow morning, so he's not late yet.'

'So in the meantime, you've got to wander around like Billy No Mates? It's unfortunate, but it can't be helped. Keep your eyes out for a suitable replacement. There must be someone with muscles up there, a lumberjack or something. Heavy snow doesn't clear itself.'

'I haven't seen anyone. Most of the people are much older than me. They're really friendly, though. Last night I had dinner with a group of staff.' She recounted what she could recall of the previous evening. As she talked, things she'd forgotten started to come back—standing on a chair to sing *We Wish You a Merry Christmas* at the top of her voice, pulling Christmas crackers and getting hit on the nose by a flying plastic toy, telling Sally the dog sled tour operator about how she was praying Dirk would ask her to marry him … or had she told that to Jim, the town crier…?

'It's all a bit of a haze, to be honest,' she admitted.

'Have you spoken to Dirk, made sure he's still coming?'

'Not yet. I'll send him a message.'

'Can't you just call him?'

Maggie frowned. 'He doesn't do phones. At least, he doesn't seem to anymore.'

They had used to talk on the phone, but now that she thought about it, it had been some weeks since Dirk had picked up. He would answer her messages later, but every time she called, it would go to voicemail.

In a quiet voice, she said, 'Do you think he's going to come?'

Renee's sigh was barely audible. 'I wish I could say yes, but I don't know. From what you've described of him, he's been a bit off recently, hasn't he?'

Renee had to get to work, so Maggie called off. In the entranceway, she pulled on her boots and jacket. The splash of snow from the road didn't appear to have stained it after all, so she headed out into the bright sunlight with a renewed sense of optimism.

Outside, the road up into the woods was intriguing, but her stomach was grumbling so she headed downhill toward the village square, passing a closed-up Barney's, until she came to a pretty café on a street not far from the village hall. A handful of other customers were eating on the tables pressed against the window, so Maggie went inside.

An instrumental version of *White Christmas* was playing from speakers hung from the ceiling, and the café was filled with gentle chatter. Maggie ordered pancakes with special Lapland maple syrup and sat at the only table near the window that was free.

While waiting for her food, she watched the scene outside. It was like an animated Christmas card. She watched a group of children emerge from a cottage farther up the street, collect their sleds and run off up the hill toward a sloping area of park shrouded in snow. A couple of benches and a little bandstand on top of the low rise offered pretty views of the town which Maggie made a mental note to check out later. Right outside, three people were walking along the street, holding bamboo sticks which they were using to knock the accumulated snow off the lights hanging across the street. The lights, currently switched off, hung practically everywhere. Maggie wondered if the town was bright enough at night to see from space.

The waiter brought her pancakes and she settled in to eat. Only then did she realise that apart from herself, everyone around her was seated in a couple. The chair opposite was the only one empty.

Dirk was due to arrive tomorrow evening. It was perfectly enough time for him to settle in, and for them to enjoy Christmas together.

She tried not to listen to the conversations going on around her. She didn't want to know about other people's lives, how perfect they were, and how much fun they were having in Hollydell. She was having quiet enough fun on her own, thank you. It didn't matter that she was sitting on her own—

'Hey.'

The chair opposite rose into the air, spun around, and came down laden with a big human sitting on it backward. A heavy winter jacket made any sense of a body shape impossible to ascertain, and a scarf and Russian hat left little face for appraisal. Eyes that were the blue of a frozen lake watched her.

'I thought I recognised you. Not many people come here alone. Sorry about yesterday.'

'What?'

'The sleigh. I splashed you. George got a little

carried away on that turn.' The man grinned as though it had been nothing more than kids messing around in the park.

Perhaps she was channelling a deeper frustration, but Maggie felt her anger forming itself into bite-sized chunks.

'You should be more careful,' she snapped. 'Your toy nearly took my legs off.'

'Really sorry,' he said again. 'My name's—'

'I don't care what your name is,' Maggie said, standing up. 'You're reckless.'

'Really sorry—'

Conversation had halted and breath caught in throats. As though finding herself in the centre of a balloon, Maggie let the air expel her, and in a rush she found herself outside the café door, a vacuum of awkwardness and discomfort at her back. She tucked her bag under her arm and marched off in the direction of the train station, too embarrassed to even look behind her. When a shout came, calling for her to wait, she broke into a stumbling run until she was out of sight.

The train sat at the platform, but the station was quiet, no one around. Maggie walked up the steps onto the platform and sat down on a bench free from snow.

She felt equal parts stupid and justified for her actions. She hadn't given the man to even introduce himself, let alone properly apologise. The sleigh hadn't really come close enough to risk cutting her legs off: cars passed closer every day in Cambridge while she was walking on the pavement. Her overreaction had come from a frustration at being alone and being embarrassed in front of all those other customers.

Or had she been the one embarrassing herself? It had already become a haze of uncertainty.

The guy was still a jerk, though. He'd sat backward on the chair, for Heaven's sake. What kind of person did that except a jack-the-lad with no responsibilities?

Maggie shook her head. She needed Renee's opinion on it all, but first she needed to call Dirk. Dirk, her boyfriend, and potential fiancé; Dirk who worked in the city with his six-figure salary (when you counted the possible bonuses); Dirk who would soon be driving around in a brand new Mercedes.

Dirk, who didn't live with her, rarely returned her calls, and hadn't even seen her in six weeks.

Naturally, he didn't answer when she called.

She tried again, four more times, the fourth time standing on the bench with the phone held up in the air to make sure it picked up the single bar of reception.

When he didn't answer, she sent him a message.

Just wanted to make sure you're all set for tomorrow? I'm here now, settling. It's perfect, everything we could have dreamed of. I can't wait to see you. We'll have such a good time XXX.

She paced up and down the platform while waiting for a reply. At the end, she watched a man in a thick winter jacket walking along the edge of the frozen lake, carrying a fishing rod in one arm and what appeared to be a mallet in the other.

On the third lap, her phone pinged.

Sorry, Pretty Pea, was in a meeting. No Christmas here, all aboard for the New Year!

She stared at the message, her neck and cheeks flushing. Did that mean he wasn't coming? Or did it just mean he wasn't thinking about Christmas at work? And there were no kisses at all this time.

She was still mulling it over when her phoned pinged again.

All good, Pretty Pea. I'll see you tomorrow! I hope you've got our cottage looking nice! Can't wait to get my teeth into a bit of that Christmas cheer!

She frowned again. The message was so unlike Dirk she could almost believe someone else had written it. It was as though Dirk had left his kindness and sensitivity behind in Cambridge when he headed off to London. No kisses at all, and what exactly was he hoping to get his teeth into? Did he actually mean Hollydell, or was his meaning something seedier?

She stared at her phone, feeling a sudden urge to dash it against the platform.

A loud banging made her look up. The man with the fishing rod was standing out on the ice, breaking a hole in it with a mallet. She stared. He was crazy. Only half of the lake was iced over; it couldn't be that thick, and if really wanted to fish, why not go down to the far end and just cast into the water?

Ignoring the fisherman, she looked back at her phone. If Dirk had time to message her, that must mean he was free to talk. She stood on the bench again and tried to call. Three times, she was put through to voicemail. The third time, she left a message.

'Dirk, I just want to hear your voice. It's really

Christmasy here and I want you to share it with me. Please just give me a quick call.'

As soon as she had hung up, she wanted to slap herself. Was it possible to sound any more desperate? Dirk would hear her message and wonder if she was going out of her mind. It wouldn't surprise her at all if he was heading home right now to unpack his bags.

Her phone pinged.

Sorry, Pretty Pea, in another meeting. I'll see you tomorrow, ok? x

A solitary kiss this time. That meant he was angry with her. Maggie sat down on the bench, her head in her hands.

She needed to call Renee. Her friend always knew what to do. She pulled out her phone, but as she went to make a call, she realised her remaining battery icon was down to the red. In the shock at having a cottage without internet access, she had forgotten to put her phone on charge yesterday, and the cold had done its work on what was left. She was down to three percent. If Dirk sent another message, she would need the remaining battery to pick it up.

She walked to the end of the platform again, and looked out at the lake. The fisherman was still on the ice, but she could see how his footprints made a line along what looked like a circular path before going out on to the ice.

Dirk might have something more to say. She would make a circuit of the lake, and if no more messages came, she would head back up to the village.

Her mind set, she started out. She had nearly

reached the point where the fisherman had gone out on to the ice when he turned around to look at her, raising a hand in greeting.

The coat was different, but the hat was the same.

'Hey,' Henry said. 'You fancy a spot of ice fishing?'

Maggie felt her anger rising. This was the man who had sprayed her with snow and then humiliated her in a busy restaurant.

'You should be careful out there,' she said. 'You don't want to fall through the ice.'

Henry grinned. He lifted a foot and stamped it down hard. 'Don't worry; all safe.'

Maggie started. The guy was clearly a fool, perhaps a genuine village idiot. All these little rural communities had one. She shook her head.

'What are you trying to do, catching fish in winter anyway? Won't they be hibernating?'

He laughed. Now she felt like an idiot. She took a few steps forward.

'Salmon don't hibernate,' he said. 'They're nervous fish, so they're hiding under the ice. Over the last few days a cold front came in, which puts them into a state of inactivity. With the weather clearing, they'll be thinking about food again.' He spread his arms. 'And here I am.'

'Not if you fall through the ice.'

He stamped his foot again. 'Perfectly safe.'

Maggie took a few steps forward, through a bank of reeds poking up through the snow. She felt an overwhelming urge to start an argument with this man, first to point out he was an idiot, and then perhaps to dredge up her frustrations with him. None of it, of course, would be because she was angry at Dirk. None of it at all.

She took one more step, and realised he was standing on the end of a snow-covered wooden pier stretching out into the water. As she tested it with her foot, he grinned.

'See? Perfectly safe.'

'I didn't see it,' she snapped.

'It's easy to miss. What are you doing down here anyway? Most guests stay up in the village. I thought you were doing some elaborate stretching exercises until I saw your phone. You ought to toss that thing into the lake. It'll save you a lot of trouble in the long run.'

'What do you know about me?' she snapped.

Henry spread his arms. 'Nothing. I'm sure there's a lot to know, though.'

'What's that supposed to mean?'

He cocked his head. 'A pretty young lady like you comes to a place like Hollydell on her own. There has to be a story there.'

'There's no story. And I'm not on my own. My fiancé is coming tomorrow night.'

He propped up his rod and turned to face her. 'Is that so? Well, I'm happy to hear that. If the two of you would like a lunch barbeque of freshwater salmon then seek me out.' He grinned. 'I'm something of a connoisseur at this time of year.'

'A connoisseur? That's a big word for a—' Maggie clamped her mouth shut, but it was too late. Her cheeks burned.

Henry grinned. 'For a country boy like me?'

'I'm sorry.'

'It's all good.'

'I have to go.'

She turned and fled. Henry called once for her to come back, but Maggie couldn't even look. She felt like an idiot, and wanted nothing more than to get on the next train and escape from Hollydell, leave it and her shame behind forever.

However, there weren't any trains until the evening, so an early morning glass of red and the comfort of a locked door would have to do instead. Feeling as though an avalanche was bearing down on her, she ran for her cottage.

10

MIFFY

By the time Maggie had walked back up to her cottage her thighs were burning. The hill wasn't so steep but in the snow it was tough exercise. She was pleased to have burned off her breakfast, but she figured her nervous energy had likely done that anyway.

Henry.

He had embarrassed her three times now, and in retaliation she had quite literally insulted his intelligence. She wanted to curl up and die.

She changed her mind about getting on the plonk so early, opting instead for some of the complimentary hot chocolate in her kitchen, and an hour of a cheesy Christmas DVD. Renee would have slapped her for being so uncharacteristically rude, so she resolved to hunt Henry down later and apologise. He shouldn't be too hard to find, as she had bumped into him multiple times already, and Hollydell felt like one big family.

He was still an idiot, though.

Halfway into the movie, she found her interest waning. On the way up to the cottage, she had seen a group assembling in the village square for a forest trek, and felt an urge to get out and enjoy herself at all costs. Men didn't like needy, desperate women, and if she wasn't careful, that was exactly what Dirk would find when he showed up tomorrow. Christmas was coming, and she was in a picture-perfect Christmas resort. It was time to shed the chains of her relationship and remember that she was a person all to herself.

She was just putting on her boots when she heard something scratching at the door.

A bear? A wolf? A wild pig? What kind of wildlife did they have in Hollydell, and how secure were the doors? She inched closer.

The scratching sound came again. Perhaps it had smelled food, although the only thing she had was the rest of a box of hot chocolate and some complimentary tea bags.

Unless she was the food.

She reached for the phone to call the village hall and send someone up to save her, when a quiet miaow came from outside.

Maggie let out a held breath. A cat.

The miaow came again. It quite clearly wanted to come inside, but there was no sign that the cottage came with a pet: no food bowls, no scratching towers, no cat flaps.

Her parents had three cats. They were warm, humming, comfortable cushions with legs. Perhaps she would let it curl up on her lap while she watched the rest of the DVD, then she would call Ellie and find out who it belonged to.

She opened the door. A tiny shape rushed inside, wrapping itself around her legs. Maggie looked down and saw a brown and black blur making a figure of eight around her ankles, a bell on the collar around its neck jingling. After a few rotations it paused and looked up at her, miaowing in earnest.

It was a tabby kitten, female, at a guess by what were missing. Probably no more than a few months old, just large enough to be autonomous but likely one which still curled up next to her mother at night. Maggie reached down and scooped her up. A little silver name tag attached to her collar read MY NAME IS MIFFY.

Maggie smiled. 'Aren't you supposed to be a rabbit?'

The kitten miaowed back an answer which could have gone either way.

Maggie carried Miffy through into the living room and put the kitten down on her lap. She restarted the DVD, but after a few minutes the kitten got tired of sitting down and began to climb her.

Unable to concentrate, Maggie carried Miffy through into the kitchen, but there was nothing she could give the little thing that resembled food. Clearly, the kitten didn't come with Comfort Cottage, but Maggie couldn't just put her out in the snow. Miffy must belong to someone, and perhaps they were looking for her right now.

In the hall, she called Ellie's number, but no one answered. Perhaps Ellie had gone out with the forest trekking group. Maggie put Miffy down on the floor, and the little kitten sauntered over to the wall and began scratching at a door post. Terrified of getting charged for damages, Maggie scooped the kitten up and put her into a pocket of her woollen coat as she slipped it on. Seemingly contented, Miffy settled down, her little eyes gazing out at the world around her.

'Come on, let's go and see who you belong to,' Maggie said, pulling her boots on and opening the door.

Overhead, the sky was clouding over, and a few flakes of snow drifted down through the air. At the end of her path, the road was still covered in pristine snow, except for one line of tracks heading up and around the corner. From just out of sight came the sound of someone hammering on wood.

Turning back downhill, Maggie went to the first three neighbouring houses, but her knocks received no answer. Either they were unoccupied or the residents were out at some event. Beyond them lay the first of the restaurants, but they were closed, probably until lunchtime.

She could take Miffy down to the village hall, of course, but if Ellie hadn't answered the phone it might be closed, and then she'd have to walk back up the hill. She turned in the direction of the hammering. The road arced up out of the village and into the trees. Even though the trees were too thick to provide much insight, Maggie got the sense that the road wound up toward some ridge or mountaintop. The hammering told her someone was up there, so maybe that was Miffy's elusive owner.

'Come on,' she said to the little cat, still peering out of its pocket. 'Let's get you home.'

She followed the line of footprints as they led up the hill. Made by boots, she realised they went both ways, as though someone had come down the hill and then walked back up again, but had attempted to walk in the same footmarks to disturb as little of the snow as possible.

Two thoughts came to mind: they had been made by a playful child, or a weirdo.

She paused for a moment before deciding to carry on. The idea of a weirdo didn't fit what she'd seen of Hollydell so far—although Henry came close. She patted the pocket containing the kitten. 'You'll protect me, won't you, Miffy?' The kitten miaowed in reply. Again, her answer could have gone either way.

Within a couple of minutes, she was enclosed in forest, but like everything else in Hollydell, it was bright and welcoming. She could imagine that if she turned off the road and hiked into the trees, eventually she'd come across a group of elves dancing around a campfire rather than a pack of hungry wolves or bears. Just in case Scotland was infested with packs of bears—did bears even live in packs?—she decided not to take the risk. She could still hear the tinkle of Christmas music, while the hammering had gotten louder.

She turned a bend in the road and found a homestead set out in front of her.

A two-storey farmhouse decked out in Christmas regalia was the main building, but beside it a lane led into a yard surrounded by outhouses. It looked like a farm except for the absence of any fields nearby. Was this the reindeer farm she had heard about? It was possible, despite the absence of any reindeer.

The hammering was coming from the largest outhouse. The line of footprints led up to the farmhouse's front door, but there was another set leading out again, through a gate and down the lane, ending at the door into the building from which the noise came. Maggie imagined the occupant had walked down to the village for breakfast before coming back to start work.

She went up to the door, knocking lightly on it. When she received no answer, she opened it a crack and peered inside.

'Hello?'

A man in overalls was leaning over a workbench. Not far away, something about the length of two cars was covered with a grey sheet. As she watched, the man put down a hammer and picked up a saw from a table next to the bench. With a grunt, he began cutting away at something out of Maggie's sight.

'Excuse me?'

The man jerked, turning around. Maggie stared. Sweat stood out on a head that was mostly bald, but he had the most luxurious white beard she had ever seen. You couldn't have bought a better one from Amazon. Rosy cheeks only made it look whiter as it bunched over his chest. He lifted an eyebrow as he pushed spectacles up his nose.

'Can I help you, Miss?'

'I'm so sorry to bother you,' Maggie said. 'I'm

staying in Comfort Cottage. The first one down the hill on the right?'

The man put down the saw and leaned back on the bench. He picked up a rag from the table and wiped his brow.

'Oh, yes. Ellie said. You're the new guest. Maggie Coates, isn't it?'

'That's right.' Maggie smiled. 'Wow, it seems everyone knows everyone here in Hollydell.'

The man laughed, a deep boom that echoed through the building. 'Well, that's partly true, but even more so here. You see, Ellie's my wife. She's actually still at home. It's her morning off. I went down to fetch her some pancakes for breakfast, but she's possibly still in bed, likely trying to sleep through the noise I'm making. I've got to get these repairs done, you see. Ellie's always telling me I leave things to the last minute. Isn't that what everyone does, though?'

Maggie smiled. 'Yes, I guess that's right.'

'Oh, I'm sorry.' The man wiped his hands on a different cloth and offered one to Maggie. 'I'm Simon. At least, that's what everyone around here calls me.'

'Nice to meet you ... Simon.'

A funny feeling had come over Maggie. There was something about the beard, and the shape under the sheet, that the overalls couldn't hide. She smiled to herself, giving a little shake of the head.

'Were you looking for Ellie?'

Maggie started, shaking the feeling off. 'Oh, no. I, um, I found a cat.'

She reached into her pocket and lifted Miffy out.

The cat nestled neatly in the palm of her hand, purring quietly, its eyes looking around the room, showing no fear at all.

'She was outside my door,' Maggie said. 'She's got a nametag and collar, so she's not a stray. Miffy, she's called, apparently.'

Simon came over and gave the little kitten a pat on the head. Up close, he smelled of mince pies.

'Sweet little thing, isn't she?' he said.

'Do you know who she might belong to?'

Simon nodded. 'Of course. This will be one of Henry's. He's the town's resident cat lady.'

Maggie stared. 'The what?'

Simon laughed. 'Well, not really a cat lady, is he? Although he does have six. He's a wonder with animals. He's a trained veterinarian, although there's not much need for one in Hollydell. Instead he runs the reindeer farm, as well as taking in any lost or stray animals. He does his best to find homes for them, but there are a few who melt his heart enough to keep them. Such a softy, is Henry. Have you met him yet?'

Maggie smiled. 'Oh, I think I bumped into him,' she said.

'If you like you can leave the kitten with me and I'll see he gets home. Although, if you fancy a walk, you could return her yourself.'

Maggie hesitated a moment. She was still digesting the information that Henry was not only a maniac sleigh-rider and an ice-fisherman, but also a cat lady.

'Where does he live?'

Simon pointed. 'Follow the track. You'll come to a

fork a little farther along. Right goes to a lookout point farther up the hill, but take the left. It loops back around to the other side of Hollydell. You'll see the reindeer farm. You can't miss it.' He smiled. 'There are reindeer.'

'Thanks.'

Simon looked keen to get back to work, but Maggie hesitated before leaving. She had an overwhelming urge to ask what was under the grey sheet.

'Are you staying until New Year?' Simon asked, breaking the silence.

Maggie shook her head. 'I go back on the twenty-seventh.'

'Oh, that's a shame. Christmas is pretty busy for many of us, but over New Year we let our hair down a bit.'

Maggie knew Simon was being ironic, but she found herself smiling. 'I'll think about it. My boyfriend is arriving tomorrow, so I'll see what he says.'

'Tomorrow?' Simon raised an eyebrow. 'Pretty girl like you, I'm surprised he wasn't here waiting for you.'

He let out a bellow of laughter that put Maggie at ease, even though the doubts surrounding Dirk and his "will he, won't he" approach had surfaced again. She bid him good day and headed off to deliver the cat. If she was lucky, she would get there before Henry returned from the lake and could leave Miffy in a back garden or somewhere without having to see him at all.

Avoiding him would definitely be for the best.

11

THE REINDEER FARM

As Maggie headed up the road from Simon's place, she quickly realised that there was no way Miffy could have walked all the way to her cottage from the reindeer farm. She had been walking for ten minutes through snow before she even reached the fork in the road, and it was another fifteen minutes after that before the trees opened out again and she saw a cluster of farm buildings and animal enclosures on a gentle hillside in front of her. Through the trees lower down the slope, she saw that indeed she had walked in a large circle that was winding back into the village.

In her pocket, Miffy had fallen asleep. Maggie nudged the kitten, and Miffy gave a lazy yawn before settling back down. Maggie smiled. Unless Miffy had a great love of snow and adventure, someone had left her near to Comfort Cottage. Ellie, possibly? Attempting to match-make for her boorish son? It couldn't possibly have been Henry himself, unless he had superhuman powers or knew a secret way up to her cottage from the lake. Maggie frowned, remembering the shape under the grey sheet in Simon's shed.

Don't even consider it.

She walked on. A few minutes later a quaint cottage appeared, set against a stand of trees set back from the road. It was smaller than Comfort Cottage, more like a shed which had been converted into a chalet. The front door was ajar and fresh prints in the snow led up and down the path, snaking off in both directions before returning.

Maggie stopped at the end of the path leading up the door and looked down at the prints, frowning. It looked like someone had been doing something in a hurry.

'Henry?' she called. 'Are you in there? It's me. The, um, insulting woman from the lake.'

No answer.

She opened the gate and walked up to the door. 'Henry?' she called again. In her pocket, Miffy stirred, lifted her little head and peered out. 'Henry!'

The sound of feet came on the stairs, and Henry appeared. Maggie noticed with a smile that he was wearing socks with snowmen on them. She also noticed that without a hat and his pulled-up coat, he was rather handsome. Standing there on his doorstep, she felt herself blush despite the cold, but with a shrug she shook any uncomfortable feelings away. Dirk was coming tomorrow, and Dirk was twice the man this insulting, ignorant country bumpkin would ever be.

Wasn't he?

'Hi. What are you doing here?' he said, frowning.

Maggie lifted out the little cat. Miffy mewed and struggled to get out of her hands. She dropped the cat on the floor, and Miffy immediately danced to Henry, wrapping herself around his legs.

'There you are! I've been worried sick.'

Henry was on his knees, rubbing the cat between his hands. Miffy purred, massaging Henry's hands with her chin.

'I found her trying to get into my cottage,' Maggie said. 'I came across Simon and he told me you were the town's resident … cat lady.'

As soon as the word was out Maggie scolded herself for her tone, which leaned a little too far toward the cynical to be taken as a joke. For his part, Henry didn't even seem to notice. He continued to rub the cat, as though Maggie didn't even exist. She resisted the urge to berate him for what she considered bad manners. The slew of footprints in the snow now revealed a man who had been searching everywhere.

What's happening to me? He's not a bad guy. Why do I feel like being so horrible to him?

Henry stood up at last, the cat disappearing farther into the house, where it was greeted with typical catlike distain by a fat longhair sitting in the entrance to a kitchen.

Henry smiled. He had a nice smile, Maggie noted. Humble. Kind. Unassuming.

Stop it.

'Thanks for bringing her back,' he said. 'She must have climbed under the sleigh cover when I took the sleigh out last night. The cover was still in the back. I remember stopping to make a turn just down from your house—after I nearly ran you down—so she must have jumped out there. Silly thing.'

'You should be more careful,' Maggie said. 'She could have got lost in the snow.'

'I know. I'm sorry. You know cats, though. They have minds of their own.' He shrugged. 'Look, you've walked all this way out here. Can I make you some tea or something? I have to go out to check on the deer in a while, but I've got half an hour.'

Maggie felt that tingle of uncertainty, that she needed to get out of Henry's house RIGHT NOW or something bad was going to happen.

Renee's voice piped up in her head. *Bad? Are you sure it'll be bad?*

'Dirk,' she muttered.

'I'm sorry?'

'Huh? Um, nothing. Sorry, I forgot I need to go somewhere.'

'Can I walk you?'

'No!'

She turned and fled before Henry could persuade her. She needed to get away from him, to be somewhere else before her tongue got her into more trouble. He was calling her from the doorway as she reached the gate. She stretched for it, using it to guide her out on to the road … and fell flat on her face, a piece of the gatepost held uselessly in her hand.

She wiped snow out of her eyes and looked up into

Henry's concerned face. He ran a hand through his hair and gave a little shake of his head.

'It broke,' he said. 'The hinge is rusted through. I hadn't got around to fixing it yet.'

Maggie opened her mouth, wanting some ice-pick-sharp barb of a dress-down to launch itself from her tongue, embed itself into his kindly heart and poison him from the inside out so he would stop looking at her with those warm, gentle eyes … but her mouth felt full of dry ice, and all she could do was take his hand and let him help her up.

'I should have warned you,' he said.

'I shouldn't have run off,' she said.

He smiled.

She smiled.

'Tea?'

Henry laughed. 'Sure. I just boiled the kettle.'

The sky had cleared, the sun returning. Henry made two cups of tea and carried them out on to a rear veranda where a wooden umbrella kept the snow off a picnic table that looked out over a pasture sloping down toward a river valley. A perfect blanket of snow had become a trampled mess, the culprits a herd of reindeer bunched together in the field's far corner.

Maggie sat down on a varnished plank of wood that was surprisingly warm. 'I'm Maggie,' she said, after Henry had sat down opposite.

'I know.'

'I know you know, but I thought it best to introduce myself again. You know, so I can pretend that I'm meeting you for the first time.'

'Why would you want to do that?'

'Well, because our first few meetings were somewhat … awkward.'

Henry shrugged. 'Nothing's ever normal here in Hollydell. You'll get used to it.'

'I'm only here for a few days.'

Henry smiled. 'Ah, but you'll never really leave. No one who comes here does. Something my mother told me once, when I was young, was that Hollydell was built from the pieces of a million different hearts. Everyone who visits leaves a piece behind, adding to the village's magic.'

'Is Hollydell really magic?'

Henry shrugged. 'I'll ask you again in a couple of days. By then you'll know for yourself.'

They sat in silence for a while, but it wasn't an awkward silence, rather a comforting one: two people at ease with each other's company.

Finally, Maggie said, 'I got the wrong impression of you.'

'Oh, really? How was that?'

'I thought you were a buffoon. Kind of bumbling and stupid, like a bear.'

Henry laughed. 'You don't hold back, do you?'

Maggie felt her cheeks redden. 'I'm not the best with words.'

'I can see that. But words, like everything else, can be learned.'

'You sound like a poet.'

Henry just shrugged again. 'I guess I'm inspired by

my surroundings. Especially at this time of year, just before Christmas. The magic is in the air, isn't it?'

'I guess.' She lifted her cup to take another sip, but found it was empty. She wanted to ask Henry for another, but Dirk's face flashed into her mind, paralysing her with a sudden guilt.

'I ought to go,' she stammered. 'I should let you get back to your work. I enjoyed the tea. Thank you.'

Henry smiled. 'Anytime. I need to make my rounds of the fields, check on the stock. Maybe later I can introduce you to some of the animals. You've already met one of my cats.'

'Um, sure.'

'Great. Well … by the way, if you're at a loose end this evening, there's a concert down in the square. Nothing massive, just a bit of a warm-up for the main event in a couple of days. A bit of music, some dancing. Perhaps I'll see you there?'

A *yes* formed on Maggie's tongue, but she bit down on it before it could escape. It was far too much like a date for a woman expecting her potential fiancé to arrive tomorrow. 'I might make it down,' she said. 'I'll see what else I've got on.'

Henry nodded, but his eyes told her the truth. She would be there, whether it was morally ethical to be there or not.

12

TUG-OF-WAR

'Maggie ... it's my lunch hour. I really needed to get into town to drop off the Christmas charity box at the homeless shelter and you know I can't use a phone while driving.'

'I'm sorry, Renee. I just really needed to talk to you. My word, I feel like a little girl....'

'Oh. Wait. I'll put you on speakerphone. That's okay, isn't it?'

'I believe so.'

There was a rustle of activity from Renee's end. Maggie sipped her cup of tea and made herself comfortable on the telephone table. The words were stumbling over themselves, but she concentrated on ordering them correctly before unleashing them on her unsuspecting best friend.

'Right, I'm in position, Mags. Shoot.'

'There's a guy ... he's really nice but I keep treating

him like dirt … he breeds cats and reindeers … and I think his dad is Santa Claus.'

Maggie went on for a few seconds longer before she realised the only sound coming from the other end was Renee's laughter.

'Oh, Maggie, is this a set-up?'

Maggie took a deep breath. 'No. I'm serious. I told you I sounded like a little girl.'

'Well, nothing like a holiday romance, is there? Is Santa's son good-looking?'

'Yes—I'm not sure he's Santa's son, it just looks like it. I mean, that would make him an elf, or a ghost, or something—'

'Calm down. It's a holiday village. They're probably all actors.'

'Wasn't it you who told me I should believe in magic?'

'Yeah, but in Christmas magic, not like proper magic like Harry Potter has.'

'What's Harry Potter got to do with it?'

'Is he there too? Perhaps he's like this guy's cousin or something?'

'No! Are you making fun of me?'

Renee laughed again. 'No, of course I'm not. It's just that this is perfect, don't you see?'

'No. It's a nightmare.'

'You're happy. That was the magic. Oops, copper at the traffic light. Better stop talking or he'll think I'm crazy. Actually, I'll just put a CD on for a minute.'

Maggie held the phone away from her ear as a crackly *Merry Christmas Everyone* by Shakin' Stevens came blaring out of the headset, accompanied by Renee's wailing karaoke rendition. After a few seconds of pure aural agony, it cut off.

'Safe. We're past him now. He gave me a wink though, cheeky devil. I wish I'd picked his serial number. I could have looked him up on the internet. He was only about twenty-five....'

'Renee? Can we deal with my situation first?'

'What situation? Come on, Mags. You met a guy. He's awesome. He invited you to some dance or whatever. You'll go, of course. What else is there to debate?'

'Dirk.'

Renee let out a sound like a deflating tyre. 'Oh, there it is. The mood killer. Have you spoken to him?'

'Briefly this morning. He didn't have time to speak because he told me he had a meeting.'

Renee growled. 'It's Christmas and he doesn't want to speak to you? How many times did he call you "Pretty Pea"?'

Maggie frowned. 'It was three or four, I think.'

'It's a cover. There's something going on. When is he due to arrive?'

'Tomorrow.'

Renee squealed. For a moment Maggie thought her friend had bumped her car. 'You could make them fight over you, proper rolling around in the snow. Do you think you could get them to both wear Christmas hats?'

'Renee, be serious.'

'Maggie ... relax. It'll be fine. Dirk will show up, live up to his name and spoil the holiday, and the new guy will be waiting with open arms. It's perfect. It's like a story.'

'I love Dirk.'

'So you keep telling yourself. I'm not convinced. I'm sure you might have once, back before he really shed his skin and became the lizard we all know and try to stamp on today, but admit it, if he doesn't show, you won't be entirely unhappy, will you?'

'Of course I will!'

But, even as she said it, Maggie began to have doubts.

'You're having doubts, aren't you?'

'No!'

'You always were stubborn. Stop looking with your eyes, and start looking with your heart. And if that fails, at least look with your stomach. Can he cook?'

'I don't know! His brother can.'

'Oh, he has a brother?' Another squeal. 'A shame I've got the children's home Christmas dinner. Oh well, maybe next year.'

'I'd love it if you came. Everyone here is in a couple. I feel so weird.'

'Well, enjoy it, because it won't be for much longer. When's he due to arrive and ruin everything?'

'Tomorrow. And he won't—'

'Well, enjoy it until then. See this as your chance to learn about yourself. Look, Mags, I've seen you sitting like a frog under a rock for years. If the rock's not Dirk and whatever whim he has going on, it's that dragon you work for. It's time to step out from under the rock and become a butterfly. Become you.'

'Frogs don't become butterflies.'

'It was an analogy. Is that the right word? And I don't mean you look like a frog, either. Well, maybe without makeup—'

'Renee!'

'Just joking. You know, laugh? What I'm saying is, forget about Dirk until he shows up. Enjoy yourself doing things for you for once. Want to go forest trekking? Do it. You don't have to worry about Dirk whining about getting his shoes dirty.'

'He wouldn't—'

'Oh, forgotten that hike we went on last year already? It wasn't even a mud path. It was gravel. And if you want to go to this dance thing, go. No need to worry about Dirk sitting in the car the whole time on some stupid business call.'

'He wouldn't do that either!'

Renee sighed. 'You have a short memory, Mags. When we went to that pantomime last Christmas and he really had to take that oh-so-important call?'

'He didn't miss the whole thing.'

'Only three quarters. And then he's sat there for the last twenty minutes all "Who's this?", "What's he doing?", as though it wasn't a silly pantomime and they haven't had the same plot for literally, like, forever. Wow, perhaps you were in love. I mean, you're pretty blind. He got his nickname for a reason, and not just because of its convenient rhyme. You know, don't you, that the first time you introduced us he asked me pronounce it with a long A sound like "Dahk", as though he were super posh or something. Perhaps that why he moved to

London, because you can't pronounce an I sound like an A the way you're supposed to.'

'Renee—'

'I've got to go. I'm at the shelter now, and I have to get back or I'll get in trouble. Well, actually I won't, because I'm a volunteer and they're grateful I show up at all, but you get the picture. I've got to get going. Keep me posted, though. Call me tonight if you can. I'll be waiting by the phone.'

'Love you, Ren.'

'Love you too, Hun. Hang in there.'

As soon as the phone clicked off, Maggie felt totally alone again. If only Renee were here, she could make everything better.

'Come on, Maggie,' she muttered. 'Let's do it then. Let's be me.'

She stood up and pulled on her boots. Outside, it had begun to snow lightly. Maggie buttoned up her coat and headed downhill toward the village square, unsure what she was doing or where she was going, hoping only to shed from her shoulders the weight of Dirk's impending appearance and her growing attraction to Henry before the weight became too great to bear, and she found herself lying face down in the snow, slowly being buried.

13

LOOKOUT POINT

DOWN IN THE SQUARE, A GROUP OF PEOPLE WERE putting up Christmas lights. As Maggie wandered past, Phillip, the delicatessen owner, called Maggie over, so for a while she held the foot of a ladder while Phillip strung a line of candle-shaped bulbs along his shop front. Phillip hummed to himself the whole time, gently contented with his work, despite a broken string of lights in a basket at his feet.

'Frost damage,' he had told her when she asked, then shrugged his shoulders. 'Can't be helped, can it?'

As they worked, several people waved and smiled as they walked past. Maggie began to wonder if she was the only person in Hollydell who wasn't blissfully happy.

'So, are you travelling alone?' Phillip said, climbing down the ladder after fixing the last light.

'My boyfriend's coming tomorrow,' Maggie said, remembering that Phillip had left early the previous night, before she had drunkenly spilled her problems to anyone who would listen.

'Oh, that'll be nice. He'll be in time for Christmas, then. It's pretty spectacular here in Hollydell. The event of the year, to be sure.'

'I can't wait,' Maggie said, perhaps with less enthusiasm than she intended.

Phillip looked about to say something else, but a voice hailed Maggie from across the street. She turned to see Ellie beckoning to her. She said goodbye to Phillip and headed over.

'Did you eat lunch yet?'

'Um, no, not yet.' Maggie glanced at her watch, and was surprised to see it was already half past one. She had completely forgotten to eat.

'Well, get this down you on the way.' Ellie handed her a wrapped sandwich. 'Beef and mustard with a sprinkling of Christmas spice.'

'Sounds, um, delicious. Where are we going?'

Ellie grinned. 'You look like a bit of a snow-shoer, Maggie.'

'I've never tried.'

'Ah, don't worry. Just imagine you're walking with tennis rackets tied to your feet. Ever try that as a kid?'

Maggie grinned. 'Probably.'

'There you go, then. A group of us are heading up to the lookout to watch the Christmas lights come on. We have to launch this year's Christmas star.'

Maggie frowned. 'What's that?'

'You'll see. Are you dressed warmly enough?'

'I think so.'

Ellie patted her on the back. 'Let's go, then. The others are waiting.'

A group of ten people had assembled outside the village hall. Gail, the catering assistant Maggie remembered from Barney's, was handing out snowshoes and giving a tutorial on how to put them on. Ellie waved at Maggie, and Gail found her another pair from a box. They weren't unlike tennis rackets: a kind of net fitted into a lightweight steel frame with a curved front end and a slightly wider back. They fitted neatly over Maggie's boots, securing with a pair of straps.

'This way,' Ellie said, waving for the group to follow. Gail waved goodbye as Ellie led them across the road and through a gate into a triangular field behind the closest line of restaurants. Children's play equipment was half-buried in snow. A cleared path arced up through the park and into the trees. Maggie, finding the shoes harder to walk in than she had expected, was last.

The path led gently uphill through tall pines. Snow had drifted on the forest floor, covering everything in a silvery blanket. From up ahead, Maggie heard Ellie's voice drifting back, telling the nearest members of the group about the care and maintenance of the forest, before going on to explain what kind of animals they were likely to spot. Maggie was happy to hear confirmation that there were neither bears nor wolves, though the mention of a wildcat was a little unnerving, even though at this time of year it was unlikely to be seen during the day.

'Where are you from, dear?' said an older lady, slowing to let Maggie catch up. 'Len and I come up from Bristol every year. Hollydell's a wonderful place, isn't it?'

Maggie, huffing far more than she'd have expected from a gentle slope—*Perhaps Dirk thinks I've got fat?!*—came up alongside her.

'Cambridge,' she said.

'Oh, do you work in the university?'

Maggie winced. 'Next,' she said.

'Next door? Oh, it must be a lovely view.'

The storefront of Maggie's workplace had a lovely view of Carphone Warehouse across the street, but there was a spire of something just about visible over the second-storey roof.

'Oh, it is,' she said, smiling. 'Not the best, but could be worse, couldn't it?'

'I'm Linda, by the way,' the old woman said. 'Len and I are both retired schoolteachers. Len came across this place years ago while researching a project for his pupils. Amazing they don't advertise it properly, isn't it? But then, if there were too many people, it would spoil it.'

Maggie nodded along, trying not to huff too loudly. The path had steepened, and walking on snowshoes was like wading through wet sand.

Up ahead, Ellie had brought the front of the group to a stop. Puffing like the Hollydell Express, Maggie came up last, and found herself in a quaint forest glade where several picnic tables stood.

'Break time,' Ellie announced. 'Roll out the gingerbread men.'

Several members of the group let out a cheer.

Maggie smiled, but she was still trying to get her breath back.

It was clear that for some members of the group, this was a regular ritual. Two couples spontaneously burst into a breathless rendition of *White Christmas*, while the others laid out biscuits and poured hot coffee out of flasks into paper cups.

'Are you here alone?' Linda said, coming to sit beside Maggie, who was perched on the end of a bench, looking out into the forest.

Maggie suppressed a sigh. 'My boyfriend's coming tomorrow.'

'Oh? So late? He'll miss so much fun.'

'I know. He's working, though. He got a promotion this year and it's taking up a lot of his time.'

'A shame he can't take time off for Christmas,' Linda said. 'I mean, everyone needs a refresh, don't they? And letting you come up here on your own … well, who knows who you might meet when magic's in the air?'

Maggie tried not to think about Henry, but his face kept flashing in her mind. Perhaps it would be better to stay at home tonight rather than meet him at the concert. It could only lead to trouble, and while it might amuse Renee to have two men fight over her, Maggie didn't see the appeal.

Ellie passed a metal container of gingerbread men down to Maggie. No chance to offer Christmas cheer had been missed; even the tin had a pretty Christmas scene on it.

'Maggie's hoping her boyfriend will propose,' Ellie

said, loud enough for the rest of the table to hear. 'Wouldn't that be a wonderful Christmas gift?'

Maggie cringed as the rest of the table oohed and aahed. She wished a sinkhole would open up in the snow to swallow her up. She wondered if there was enough time to run back to her cottage, collect her things and make it to the train before Andrew began the daily journey to Inverness.

'How long have you been together?' someone asked.

Maggie had to think about it. 'Four years,' she said at last, even though she'd only count the year he'd been in London as a half.

'Well, I guess it's due,' Linda said.

A couple more people shuffled closer, no doubt with questions of their own, but Ellie stood up. 'Don't hound the poor girl,' she said. 'Let's get going. We have a tight schedule.'

They packed up their things and headed on up the path, which was cutting back more and more as the hillside steepened. Maggie found herself at the back again, this time fearing avalanches rather than wildcats, despite Ellie's assertion that there was nothing to worry about.

And then, nearly two hours after setting out, they broke out of the forest and Maggie found herself on a snowy hilltop with panoramic views of Hollydell below them and the rolling forested hills surrounding it. She looked for signs of other civilization, but other than a vague grey line a couple of valleys over that might have been the railway line, there was no sign that there was anything else left in the world.

Hollydell could have been the only town left on Earth.

Maggie smiled. Rather than feeling concerned, it filled her with a wonderful sense of peace.

'Oh look, there goes Andrew,' Ellie said, pointing down into the valley.

A line of smoke puffs and a faint chug-chug indicated the train moving through the forest. Maggie caught a glimpse of it through the trees as it passed alongside another small lake, then it was gone out of sight.

Linda clapped Maggie on the back. 'Only one more day, dear. Just one more day. Although if I were your young man, I'd already be here.'

Maggie forced a smile. 'He's just been so busy….'

But even as she said it, she wondered. Dirk never talked to her about what he did, he just blocked her out. She wasn't even sure what his role in the company was. He was a member of the director's board, but what did he direct?

She tried to shake off the feeling that in recent months he had acted as though she were now beneath him. Perhaps it embarrassed him to say his girlfriend worked in a clothes shop. She'd never even thought about it while he was working for his father's company, but now he'd landed a better job, she wasn't so sure.

'Okay, let's get the star launched,' Ellie said. 'Len, can you get out the balloon? David, please check the batteries. We can't have them going out before Christmas night. Maggie, you're our newest member, so you can have the honour of holding the guide rope. Just don't let go until I say.'

Maggie had no real idea what was going on. Len had taken a large, clear balloon out of a bag and was holding it by a thick cord attached to one end. The man called David was holding a plastic star with a light bulb inside. He pressed a button on the side and it illuminated brightly enough to make Maggie wince.

'I have no idea how this doesn't get you in trouble with the aviation authorities,' Linda was saying to Ellie, but Ellie just shrugged and laughed.

'We got it cleared,' she said. 'We're not on any flight paths here anyway. The only thing you're likely to see in the skies over Hollydell is Santa's sleigh.'

Even though a couple of the group laughed heartily, Ellie had said it with such conviction that Maggie could believe it had been a statement, not a joke. She thought of the shape in Simon's shed hidden by the grey sheet, then shook her head.

No. It was ridiculous.

'Okay, we're all ready,' Len said.

'Switch it on,' Ellie said to David, who flicked the switch, illuminating them all. Maggie hadn't realised how dark it had been getting until she saw how lit up their faces were, but the sun was close to the horizon already.

'Okay, let go. Maggie, on three … one, two … three!'

At Ellie's indication, Maggie let go of the rope. The star, hanging below the helium balloon, drifted gently up into the sky until it was little more than a distant speck. With a creak, the cord, tied around a metal hook embedded into a large rock, went taut, and everyone broke into a spontaneous rendition of *When you Wish upon a Star*, clapping along as they sang. Maggie, caught off guard, joined in by the end of the first verse, and by the time the song finished, she was singing as loud as anyone.

To the west, the sun was beginning to set.

Ellie stepped out of the group and clapped her hands. 'Well done, everyone. Hollydell's Christmas star is officially launched. Now, we need to make haste. We have about an hour to get off this mountain, an hour to eat dinner and get changed if you need it, then it's time for the snowman concert in the village square. Are you all ready?'

A series of cheers rose up.

Ellie frowned. 'Oh, I forgot something. How silly of me.' She lifted a large flask up on to the rock. 'The hot mulled wine. What a silly woman I would have been to carry this straight back down again. Cups out, everyone!'

The cheers this time were even louder. Maggie couldn't help but laugh. Surrounded by such joy and enthusiasm in an atmosphere drenched in Christmas magic, it was easy to put Dirk out of her mind.

She took an offered cup and waited until Ellie raised a toast. 'To Christmas, and joy to everyone!' Ellie said.

Glancing up at the star hanging high above them, Maggie saw it had begun to flash.

14

THE SNOWMAN CONCERT

WITH THE SUN SET, MAGGIE WONDERED HOW THEY were going to negotiate their way back down the forest path in near-darkness. She hadn't noticed Ellie or any others carrying torches with them, and she hadn't even brought her smartphone to use its light. They had gone no more than a few steps under the trees though when a line of fairy lights Maggie hadn't previously noticed blinked on, illuminating the meandering path with a dim but colourful glow.

'Oh, how pretty,' Linda said.

'Must cost a fortune,' Len grumbled, but in front of them, Ellie laughed.

'Solar panels,' she said, clapping him on the shoulder. 'And light sensor timers. We're pretty high-tech here in Hollydell.' She turned and winked at Maggie. 'Well, that's what we tell people. Actually it's fairy dust.'

They continued on down through the illuminated tunnel the path had now become, moving in single file, their snowshoes padding softly over the snow pressed down by their ascent. Somewhere along the way, Ellie started singing, and by the time they emerged at the top of the park where they had set off, they had sung their way through pretty much every Christmas carol Maggie knew.

Gail was waiting outside the village hall to collect their snowshoes, clearing the snow off with a brush and stacking them into a box. They had descended far quicker than Maggie would have believed during their arduous upward trek, and even though night had fallen, it was still shy of five o'clock. She remembered today was the winter equinox, though as Ellie cheerfully pointed out, 'From tomorrow we're counting down until summer.'

The concert was due to start at seven. Linda and Len invited Maggie and a couple of others to meet them at six o'clock for dinner in a little restaurant called The Elf House, which served Christmas dishes from all over the world.

'Ain't nowhere tastier in town,' Len said. 'And we've tried them all.'

Maggie gratefully accepted, then excused herself. For reasons even she couldn't quite understand, she headed down the hill to the train station and climbed up on to the platform just a few minutes before the train was due to arrive. She took a seat at the far end, in the shadows where she wouldn't be seen unless she made herself known.

It was a long shot, but perhaps Dirk had decided to come early in order to surprise her. And if he did, she would surprise him by being here waiting. They could eat with Len and Linda, then retire to Comfort Cottage to have a quiet night together with a DVD and hot chocolate.

Perfect.

But when the train rolled in and a handful of people disembarked, Dirk was not among them.

Maggie waited until Andrew had switched off the train's lights, shut down its boiler, and headed up to the village.

She needed to speak to Dirk, just to make sure he was coming. He hadn't wanted to talk yesterday, but it was nearly Christmas. Surely his company couldn't be so busy that he couldn't spare her a few minutes? At the very least she could send him a message.

But when she reached into her jacket pocket for her phone, she remembered leaving it behind in the cottage.

She bumped her head back against the wall and smiled. It actually felt good to have no way to contact him, as though she had bitten through a leash. The sense of freedom was uncanny.

So, she would have to wait until he arrived tomorrow, or come back down here to call him, by which time it would likely be too late, and he would be asleep, getting an early night before the long journey to Hollydell tomorrow.

And in the meantime, she had a pseudo-date with Henry.

A tingle of guilt tickled through her. Perhaps she should go back to the cottage, ring Renee and lament her problems, then stand Henry up and feel relieved of her guilt toward Dirk.

Or she could go up the village and a have a good time, allow Hollydell's magic to do its work.

She stood up and walked across the platform until she could see the sky above the village.

The Christmas star they had launched from the hilltop was twinkling against the background of the night sky like a miniature firework.

'Come on, Maggie,' she muttered, clenching a quietly resolute fist. 'Let's do this.'

Len and Linda were waiting at a corner table. Three other people Maggie hadn't met before were also dining with them. Linda pulled out a chair for her then introduced the others. The two older men were John and Ted, a couple from Birmingham who had been coming to Hollydell every year since John had retired four years ago. And Emma was a university professor from Plymouth who was 'single and proud, although if Santa came knocking, I'd let him fill my stocking.' As she explained to Maggie, she taught modern poetry, although didn't have much of a flair for it herself.

Maggie enjoyed a dish of barbequed prawns and roasted potatoes, something the menu claimed was Christmas, Australian-style. On Len's insistence, they all shared a bottle of Christmas-spiced, warmed port, which went straight to Maggie's head. When they all headed out as a group to go to the evening concert,

Maggie felt rather lightheaded. Snow had begun to fall again, gently filling in the footprints left by the village's residents and touching up its cover over gardens and rooftops.

A small stage had been set up in one corner of the village square. Maggie, who had forgotten to bring her events program from the cottage, asked to borrow Emma's. Tonight's show was a rendition of *The Snowman* by Raymond Briggs, followed by a modern dance version. She found herself smiling. Hollydell, for all its traditionalisms, still had plenty of modernisation.

Wooden benches made a semi-circle in front of the stage. Maggie looked around for Henry, but he was nowhere to be seen. It was early still, and he likely had his reindeer and cats to tend to and feed before coming down. It was selfish of her to expect him to be here waiting.

'What do you think of Hollydell so far?' Emma asked, as they sat among the rest of the small crowd, waiting for the show to start.

'It's amazing,' Maggie said. 'I could never have imagined anything like this could exist in the middle of Scotland.'

Emma smiled. 'The more often you come here, the more you'll start to feel like it's not Scotland at all, but perhaps "somewhere" else, like you've time-travelled or something. Now, I don't believe in all that rubbish, but Hollydell has magical properties, for sure. I was in a dark place in my life when I first came here.'

'Is that so?'

'I was battling depression, struggling to hold my life

together. I could barely get up for work, and I was like a zombie walking around campus. I felt like my life had no meaning, like I had nothing to look forward to. It was early December and I couldn't bear the thought of another Christmas home alone. I decided I needed a holiday somewhere, and I came across Hollydell. I don't know how I found it because it wasn't listed like a regular site, it was as though it found me. Do you understand what I mean?'

Maggie nodded. 'I understand exactly.'

'I didn't know what to expect, but after I came here, it changed my life. The first time was a little nerve-racking, but once you get into the swing of things, it's amazing. You see, most people come back again and again. You'll get to know them, and you'll spend all year thinking about returning to this wonderful little community where everyone's friendly and kind. You'll share laughs and good times, and the thought of going back again the next year will make the drudgery of your life worth it. Believe me, Hollydell is a life-changing place.'

'I'm beginning to understand that.'

'I'm guessing you came here for a special reason too?'

'My relationship with my boyfriend wasn't going too well. He got a good job and moved to London, and since then, well, the long-distance thing hasn't really worked out. It's not just that, but he's now a company director, whereas I work a shop floor.'

'Nothing wrong with a good, honest job,' Emma said. 'We can't all be painting church ceilings. If you

96

love you what do, you're sorted. Money is just a number. Happiness is uncountable.'

Maggie smiled. 'I wish my boss would take her foot off my neck sometimes.'

Emma laughed. 'Yeah, I have one of those. Our university dean is a proper dragon. There's a story on campus that in the refectory they serve his toasted buns untoasted because he breathes enough fire to toast it for himself. We call him Professor Puff behind his back. Kind of like a dragon, but not a scary one.'

Maggie laughed. 'We call our boss Thundercloud. She literally never smiles, and when she enters the room, all the lights seem to dim.'

Emma slapped her thigh. 'You know what's good about those kind of people, though, don't you?'

'No, what?'

'They make you appreciate the days they're not there. Look, you just hang in there. Things will work out, or they won't, but one way or another, you'll survive. You're looking down a tunnel right now, and you can't see the end, but all you've got to do is keep driving. And when you get there, you might find you're in a better place than you were before. Oh, looks like we're about to start.'

The audience clapped as someone in a snowman costume and holding a classical guitar stepped out on to the stage. The figure bowed to the audience, then moved to the side and sat down on a chair.

Softly, the snowman began to play a finger-picking version of *Walking in the Air*. Maggie felt a tingle of electricity run down her back as the amplified notes rang out. She glanced around, hoping Henry was here to see this, but couldn't see him. Beside her, Emma was oohing and aahing as a group of people walked on to the stage. Dressed as a family, they began going through the motions of family life: eating breakfast, getting ready for work, cleaning up. One by one they left until only a young man dressed in pyjamas was left. Two stage hands pushed out a bed, and he lay down, pretending to go to sleep. A few moments later, he woke dramatically, and then peered out of a window painted on the stage back. Silently exclaiming the onset of heavy snow, he ran about the stage, before the stage back lifted to reveal a snowy garden scene.

'Do they do this every year?' Maggie whispered.

'Every couple of years,' Emma whispered back. 'They cycle through the classics. Best thing is, if you're a regular visitor, you get given a part. Linda is the mother this year.'

'I thought I recognised her.'

Maggie watched as the drama unfolded. The snowman with the guitar continued to play light, delicate background music as the boy first built a snowman, which then came alive and enjoyed the delights of his home. Then, for the flight sequence, four people came on to the stage and sang a choral version of *Walking on the Air* to the guitar accompaniment, while the boy and his snowman ran around the audience with their arms outstretched. As they swooped and dived through the benches, the crowd whooped and cheered.

Returning to the stage, the stage back lifted again to reveal a snowy forest. Several other snowmen appeared and they all danced for a while to Irish jig music. Several members of the crowd got to their feet and danced along.

The biggest cheer, though, came when Santa appeared. Rather than Simon, as Maggie had expected, it was Andrew wearing the red suit and beard, while his reindeer were Ellie and Len wearing plastic antlers.

Then, of course, came the return to the house, and the sad bit Maggie hadn't been looking forward to. However, instead of the boy waking up to find the snowman gone, when he went outside this time, the snowman was waiting with open arms. The crowd cheered. The snowman and the boy embraced. The rest of the cast members came out on to stage, and even the snowman with the guitar stood up. They all took a bow before leaving the stage as a drum kit was wheeled on. Andrew sat down behind it, and the guitar-playing snowman took up its guitar again. The man dressed as the boy—who Maggie had figured out now was Jim, the town crier—brought out a microphone.

'Let's rock it up,' he said, only slightly awkwardly.

The crowd cheered. Benches were hastily pushed away as a rock version of *Walking in the Air* kicked off.

'Nowhere else in the world could get away with such utter cheesiness,' Emma laughed. 'The first time always makes you cringe, but once you've seen it a couple of times, you'll just love it. Merry Christmas, Maggie!'

After the first song was finished, the band—joined by Gail playing bass—tore through versions of several Christmas classics. By the time they closed out with a ragged but barnstorming version of *Merry Xmas*

Everybody, the crowd was full of laughter. Everyone was covered in the snow that was falling heavily now, and backslaps and cheers were everywhere. Ellie and a couple of others were carrying around trays of drinks in paper cups. Maggie opted for a hot chocolate.

'Brilliant,' she said, when Ellie asked her about the performance. 'I've never seen anything like it.'

'We always aim to surprise,' Ellie said. 'It gets a little more slapdash every time, but it's always a lot of fun.'

As Ellie moved off into the crowd, Maggie looked around for Henry, but couldn't see him anywhere.

Something must have come up, she figured. He was busy with his farm, and no doubt he had lots of other things to prepare at this time of the year. And it was okay, because Dirk was coming tomorrow, so she couldn't really be going on dates with men she'd only just met—it wasn't right. Dirk loved her, and she loved Dirk. Henry was no one.

At least, as Linda came over and convinced her to come up to Barney's for a nightcap before the snow got too heavy, that was what she tried to convince herself.

15

STILL WAITING

'So, you had a good time, even though he stood you up?' Renee let out an exasperated puff. 'Those two statements don't belong together in the same sentence, Maggie. Work with me here. It's too early in the morning to be going against accepted social situations.'

'Ren, it's after nine o'clock.'

'And let me guess, you've already been out for a jog, built a snowman, and waved good morning to a group of dishy construction workers?'

Maggie laughed. 'One out of three's not bad. I built a snowman and I went for a walk. No construction workers, though.'

'Shame. So, Dirk's due tonight, is he?'

'On the five p.m. train.'

'Which means he should be on the way to Scotland right now, unless he's being a rich toff and flying. Have you spoken to him?'

'Not yet. I tried him but he didn't answer. His phone was probably in his bag or something.'

Renee was silent for a moment. Then she said, 'You probably ought to check he's coming. Then, based on that information, you can decide whether to be mad or relieved about the dishy guy standing you up.'

'You make me sound like a complete player.'

'I'm just giving you good, solid advice. It's always best to be in control of a situation. Like when I don't check on the Christmas tree supplier to make sure they've got a nine-footer in stock, only to find out that the best I can get is a six-footer and a table to make it look bigger.'

'Sounds like a nightmare.'

'It is. Size is important for little kids. Never cried when your brother got a bigger present, even if yours was clearly more expensive?'

'I'm an only child.'

'It was an analogy. For the record, I have. Multiple times. I'd still cry now, but my parents stopped giving us presents three years ago. Now my mother just wants to take me shopping in the sales. Sure, it's fun, but it doesn't have the same magic, does it?'

Maggie laughed. 'Not really.'

'So, you'll call Dirk?'

'I'll try.'

'Keep me posted. Look, I have to go. Got three hundred and fifty mince pies to bake this morning with an oven that only has a capacity for thirty unless you line them close enough to risk the gunge overflowing and getting then all stuck together. Perhaps I'll just make a giant one instead. Anyway, got to go. Keep smiling, Mags.'

'Will do.'

Renee called off. Maggie stared at the phone in her hand, wondering whether to call Dirk. It had been a lie that she had called him before: she had been too scared he wouldn't pick up. He should be on the Edinburgh train by now. From London it would go direct, so he'd be sitting in his reserved seat—most likely in a first class carriage, the cost of which he would claim as a business expense—reading a broadsheet newspaper. He'd always been a *Sun* person until he got his new job. Now it was always *The Times* or *The Telegraph*.

If he was really was a company director now, his phone would be beside him on the table, most likely plugged into a complimentary charger. He would have to see her call, and with the number unrecognised, he would have to pick up, in case it was business.

But what if he didn't?

What would that mean for their relationship?

She wanted to scold herself, tell herself to stop being so ridiculous. She was acting like a fourteen-year-old having a playground breakup, but she couldn't help it.

She picked up the phone and dialled his number.

It rang six times before reverting to voicemail. Dirk's cheerful voice announced his name and company and invited the caller to please leave a message.

Maggie stared at the phone. Six times. It usually rang eight before reverting. That meant Dirk had intentionally ended the call.

'I'm going crazy,' she muttered.

Dirk was sitting by the phone, had seen the number, and not wanted to answer. Perhaps he was in the quiet coach?

Maggie made up her mind. He needed to know who was calling.

There was only one thing she could do. She stuffed her smartphone into her coat pocket and headed for the train station.

A tall clock on a pole that had been decorated with fairy lights told her it was a quarter to ten as she walked past the village hall. Ellie was outside, building a snowman, and briefly hailed her.

'Don't forget, we depart at eleven!' she called cheerfully, her cheeks glowing red from the cold.

'I won't!' Maggie called, hoping her attempt to call Dirk wouldn't leave her in too much despair to make the dog sledding. She'd always wanted to try it, unreliable boyfriend or not.

The train station was quiet and deserted. A sign next to the entrance saying THANK YOU FOR VISITING PLEASE COME AGAIN flickered with fairy lights. Maggie smiled at it then climbed up on to the platform, finding her usual bench near the far end, away from anyone who might wander past.

She took a deep breath and called Dirk's number. She could barely hear the rings over her heartbeat.

Five … six … seven … eight … 'Hello, this is Dirk….'

She cut off. It had rung out this time, but he hadn't answered. It had taken her twenty minutes to make it down to the train station from Comfort Cottage, and in that length of time all sorts of things could have happened. He might have been called away, he might be talking to someone else about a job—

'He's supposed to be on a train,' she said aloud. 'He should be staring out of the window, or reading a newspaper.'

Perhaps he had fallen asleep? Maggie shook her head. Dirk didn't nap; he never had that she remembered. Any free time he had would see his head in a book or newspaper.

She opened up her messages and opened a new one to Dirk. She had hoped that after finding reception, her phone would have pinged with new messages sent while she was offline, but nothing had come through.

Are you coming? she typed, then immediately deleted it. Too forward, too accusatory. He would think she was becoming obsessive, get off the train and take the next one back.

It's wonderful here, she typed instead. *I can't wait for you to enjoy it with me. Looking forward to seeing you so much xxx.*

It was too over the top this time, so she deleted the line of Xs and instead added a flashing Christmas tree emoticon and pressed send before she could analyse it too much.

A little *sent* notification appeared next to the message, and a moment later the icon for *read* appeared. So, he was with his phone after all. Maggie stared as a box appeared with flashing periods to show Dirk was typing.

Her instinct was screaming at her to just call him while she knew he was holding his phone, but she sensed he wouldn't answer. Something had happened.

Sorry, Pretty Pea, I got stuck in an early morning meeting and I missed the train! Devastated. I'll never make the connection in Edinburgh now, so I'll try again tomorrow. It's only the 22nd, so plenty of Christmas left!

Her heart lurched as she read the message over and over. He wasn't coming today.

She called Renee, who picked up on the second ring.

'What? I've got another hundred and eighty mince pies to go. Honestly, you should see me. I couldn't be better at cooking if I wore a Wonder Woman costume.'

Maggie, trying not to cry, told Renee about Dirk's message. 'He missed the train,' she said finally, for perhaps the eighth time.

'Okay, here's what you do,' Renee said. 'You're in a perfect Christmas village. Delete Dirk's jerkisms and you're having a great time, right? Okay, apart from being stood up by the guy you weren't actually on a date with, but we'll shelve that for now. You're having a good time, aren't you?'

'Yeah, I guess so.'

'Well, ramp it up a little. Start having a better time. Start having the best time you've ever had. You've got a roster at work, right? You'll be doing the Christmas grudge shift next year, right? This is it. This is your chance to have a fantastic Christmas. So what if he's not there? You're an independent woman. At least, you are now. Channel it, Mags. Get out there and have a good time, and if he shows up tomorrow you can be all like, boo-yah, who are you?'

'Thanks, Ren,' Maggie croaked. 'I think.'

'What's next on the agenda?'

'Dog sledding.'

There was a sound like someone slapping the phone on the other end of the line.

'Dog sledding? And you're whining about Dirk not showing up? Get up there and have a good time. That's an order. Ouch! Word of warning: never use a phone while taking mince pies out of the oven.'

'I, um, won't.'

'Now … get.'

Renee hung up. Maggie stared at the phone before putting it back into her pocket. Her friend was right. She could either allow Dirk to be the thundercloud, or she could not.

'Dog sledding, here I come,' she said through gritted teeth.

16

DOG SLEDDING

'THIS ONE'S ROVER, THIS ONE'S BENNY, AND THIS one's Princess Margaret,' Sally said, pointing out the three dogs. At the chuckles of laughter, she added, 'Every year, we have a naming competition for the newest puppies. You get some old faithful, and a few surprises.'

'That one over there is Trafford,' Emma pointed out. 'Named after Lancashire's cricket ground. No idea how that slipped through the filter, but after a couple of seasons, it feels natural.'

Trafford gave a delighted bark as though to agree, then sat back on his haunches, his tongue lolling.

'And this year, we have a couple of new drivers to announce,' Sally said. 'As those of you who are regulars know, between Christmas and New Year we run short training courses for people interested in learning to drive a sled. A couple of last year's trainees have graduated to full drivers this year, so please give a hand to Ted and David.'

Both men raised a hand as the others clapped.

'Now,' Sally said, clapping her hands together as the applause died down, 'let's get going. The dogs always get a special treat at the far end of the trail, so they're always chomping at the bit to get underway.'

The sled teams were made up of six dogs. Each team pulled a sled which carried up to three people. Maggie was shown to a seat next to Linda, while Ted, their driver, sat on a seat in front. The sleds were made of lightweight steel, almost liftable with one hand.

'Isn't this exciting?' Linda said. 'It's no different to Lapland.'

'Off we go,' Ted said, shaking the reins.

As one, the dogs jumped up, running forward through the snow, jerking the sled along behind them. Powerful huskies, Maggie was surprised how quickly they sped along, following a flat trail through the trees that led east out of the village, following the curve of a hill. Their sled was in the lead, with two others following a short way back. Sally was driving the third sled, content to let the new drivers go off ahead.

After a short ride through trees, they descended a gentle slope and came out alongside the lake where Maggie had seen Henry ice-fishing. Now completely covered in ice, it was as shiny as an ice-skating rink.

'I wouldn't get any ideas,' Linda said. 'It won't support your weight. Not yet. Usually by mid-January.'

'Is Hollydell open in mid-January?'

Linda laughed. 'Of course. It's a winter wonderland right through the end of February, then things begin to calm down. Christmas is its special time, though.'

The trail rounded the lake and followed a straight path alongside a river gushing among rocks piled with snow.

'The train line used to continue out here,' Linda said. 'There was an old mining town, but it closed down, and the line closed with it. Now the old station building is our destination.'

'Bit of a historical tour, this,' Ted laughed, leaning over his shoulder.

Maggie stared out at the landscape as they bumped along. The river was a background sloshing over the jingle of bells attached to the sleds and the panting of the dogs. The forest rising up the hills to either side was snow-covered and pristine. She gave a shake of her head, still unsure how this could be Scotland.

'It's unreal, isn't it?' Linda said, as though reading her thoughts. 'We all try to deny it our first time. Just let it absorb you, Maggie. Let it be part of you.'

'I'm trying,' Maggie said.

They all fell silent, the beauty and peace of the surroundings filling them with a calm that required no words. Maggie pushed Dirk and Henry and even Renee from her mind, and concentrated on the bustling ride alongside the river.

'This is the life,' she muttered at last.

'There you go,' Linda laughed.

'We're nearly there,' Ted said, pointing up ahead. 'There's our destination.'

Maggie leaned out to look over Ted's shoulder. Up ahead, an old station building was approaching, still standing on top of an old platform next to the path. Its wooden roof was laden with snow, and a small Christmas tree decorated with lights stood outside.

Ted brought the sled to a stop.

'Thanks for riding,' he said, tipping his woolly hat. 'It was a pleasure to take you on my maiden journey.'

Sally came walking back along the line. 'Head inside, everyone. Hot chocolate and cake are waiting for you.'

'I hope you're coming to the dance tonight,' Linda said to Maggie. 'It's pretty essential to keep the weight off.'

Maggie grinned. 'I wouldn't miss it for the world.'

'Especially since we have cooking class in the afternoon.'

Maggie followed Linda inside, where they found Ellie standing beside a table laden with hot chocolate steaming in large, ornate bowls and piles of mince pies arranged on multi-level cake stands.

'Tuck in,' Ellie said, brushing some crumbs off her cheek before offering a guilty grin. 'I'm not carrying any of this back to the village.'

The hot chocolate, as everywhere in Hollydell, was luxuriously thick. Maggie treated herself to three marshmallows from a bowl and a dollop of cream, just because Renee would insist. Feeling a sudden urge to be alone, though, she carried it outside on to the old platform.

The dogs were relaxing after having their food and

drink, lounging around in a straw-filled shelter at the end of the platform. Sally was walking among the sleds, checking the harnesses, wiping accumulated ice off the runners. She didn't notice Maggie, so Maggie walked up to the far end of the platform and stood looking out at the forest closing in around them. This was the true end of the line, she realised, although a cut in the trees and a signboard indicated a walking trail. Maggie couldn't read it from this distance, but there were several pictures on the sign as though it was a circle of historical interest.

'You have to come on one of the summer tours to visit the old mining town,' a voice said from behind her.

Maggie let out a little gasp of surprise, but it was only Ted. No longer the spirited sled driver, he had reverted to his familiar role as an elderly statesman, leaning on a walking stick as he approached her.

'I was just wondering what it was,' Maggie said.

'An old mining town. Abandoned for about a hundred years,' Ted said. 'There are some interesting ruins, if that's your thing.'

'It might be,' Maggie said. 'I'm not sure.'

Ted smiled. He reminded her of her beloved grandfather who had passed three years before. His eyebrows were pure white, unkempt as her grandfather's had been, almost as though it was a right of the elderly to keep them as wild as they wished.

'You don't strike me as having the best of times,' Ted said. 'Are you all right?'

Maggie sighed. She gave a shake of her head, frustrated with her weakness, and how easily she could be disarmed.

'My boyfriend was supposed to come today,' she said. 'But he can't make it. A business meeting. He hopes to come tomorrow.'

'There's only one more train,' Ted said. 'The line is closed on Christmas Eve and Christmas Day. He's cutting it fine.'

Maggie swallowed down the urge to cry. 'I'm not sure he wants to come at all,' she said. 'He's been pretty distant since he got a new job in London. I've barely seen him these last three months.'

Ted gave a thoughtful nod. 'You know, sometimes what you think is the right thing turns out not to be,' he said. 'Your heart might be aching now, but in a month, or two months, you might struggle to recall this young man's name. Life is like that. It can strike you with disaster or immediate happiness at any time it likes.'

'I almost feel as though we've broken up without the words being spoken,' Maggie said. 'We've been together for four years. I hoped he would propose to me here. I thought Hollydell sounded like the perfect place. Somewhere full of Christmas magic, where he might feel right about it.'

'If he doesn't feel like it on the greyest, coldest, windiest day of autumn, standing in a bus shelter with wet shoes having missed the last bus to get him to work on time, having left his phone behind and realised he had a big meeting he'd forgotten all about, a bit of Christmas magic won't help,' Ted said. 'I think you're looking in the wrong place with this young man.'

Maggie shook her head. 'I don't know. Part of me doesn't even want him to come. It's like a chain, holding me back. This was my last dice roll, and it's failing. When I go to the station at five o'clock tomorrow, I don't know if I want him to be on that train or not.'

Ted nodded. 'Hollydell works in mysterious ways. It heals in ways you and I can't understand. Life is the same. You never know what will happen. Look at myself and John. I'm seventy-seven years old, lifelong single. John had two failed marriages, back before it was okay to feel as he feels. One day, on the way home from work, I felt a sharp pain in my side. It didn't go away over a few days, and so I went for a scan. I was diagnosed with cancer of the colon. Terminal.'

Maggie stared. 'Is it…?'

Ted smiled. 'I got sicker and sicker, until I could barely get around. My doctor recommended I move to a hospice. There I met John. He was my primary carer. We fell in love. Christmas was approaching, and I was hanging on, but by the end of January it was predicted I would no longer be able to walk. We decided to take a Christmas holiday together. Our last, and our first.'

The hot chocolate was going cold in Maggie's hands, so she finished it off. 'What happened?'

'Well, we had a delightful time. We did everything we could that I could manage, and when we left Hollydell just after New Year, I felt great. In my mind, I mean. We had a perfect holiday, and I'd never felt better. I still felt like my body was falling apart, but you know, the end of January came, and I could still walk about. The end of February, and I felt a little stronger. By the time summer came around, my doctor had told me that my cancer was in remission.'

'But it was terminal, wasn't it?'

'So they said. By the following December, I was given the all-clear, and we came again to Hollydell to celebrate, and we've been coming every year since. This is our fourteenth successive year, and it gets no less magic as the years pass.'

Maggie wiped a tear from the corner of her eye. 'So you think Hollydell cured you?'

Ted smiled. 'Oh, I wouldn't say that. I think I cured me. What Hollydell gave me—and what John gave me—was a reason to live. I wanted to live like I'd never wanted to live before. And here I still am, failing, but still alive.' He shrugged. 'I don't want to get all storybook on you—for all I know, I was misdiagnosed—all I'm saying is that Hollydell has a certain type of magic, but you mustn't go looking for it. John found Hollydell advertised on a crumpled piece of paper at the bottom of a supermarket shopping bag. It wanted us to come here, and it gave us the chance to truly breathe. You have to let it do the same for you. If your boyfriend doesn't show up, for whatever reason, don't hold on. Don't let it bring you down. While he might have his reasons, if he really loved you, he'd be here already. If he's not on that train tomorrow evening, see it as a sign that there is more to come.'

Maggie smiled. 'I'll try. It's just so much easier to say than do.'

'Oh, that it is for sure. But don't give up. Christmas hasn't even rolled around yet, and that's when Hollydell is the most special of all.'

'I can't wait.'

Ted laughed. 'Neither can I. My waistline disagrees though.' He patted Maggie on the arm. 'Come on, there's a ton of hot chocolate left, and Ellie has a rule. No one goes anywhere until it's all gone. Honestly, I'd swear those containers get bigger every year.'

17

FALL

Maggie had been considering opting out of the cooking class that followed the dog sledding, but after a light salad lunch in the village hall which had the sole purpose of leaving them feeling hungry, she allowed Linda and Ted to convince her. And when Ellie, who seemed to be everywhere at once, took an example of what they would be making out of the fridge and set it down on the table in front of them, Maggie knew she had made the right decision.

Chocolate log.

What better way to mend a potentially broken heart than to shamelessly overload on chocolate? And if she felt in a better mood when she was finished, she might even take a slice up to Henry to tell him she forgave him for standing her up on their not-really-a-date, something that the disappointment of Dirk's delayed arrival had clouded over.

Ellie, who seemed on a personal mission to give

them all heart attacks, insisted they test the mixture at each possible opportunity, spooning clean each bowl before washing, and keeping themselves lubricated with either more hot chocolate or hot mulled wine. Maggie, afraid she would start to look like a cacao plant, opted for the wine.

It was Christmas after all.

Finally, with her chocolate log finished and resplendent, decorated with a little snowman and a Santa on a sleigh, she sat back, feeling a little worse for wear, and gave Linda and Ted a set of high-fives.

'You're wasted in education,' said Linda, who still seemed to think Maggie worked at Cambridge University. 'There's a three-Michelin-starred pastry restaurant waiting for you to walk through the door.'

'After many days like today, I'm not sure I'd be able to walk out again,' Maggie said, patting her stomach. 'But I'll keep it in mind if I fancy a change in career.'

Needing to shed the day's calories while she still could, Maggie bid the cooking group farewell and headed out, her chocolate masterpiece in a box under her arm. It was just after three o'clock, with an hour or so of decent daylight remaining. Emma had gleefully informed her that after the dance in the village square, there was a buffet and Christmas karaoke night at Barney's.

Afraid of enjoying herself too much, she decided some physical punishment was in order before she filled her stomach with more delicious Christmas food. There were various nature trails around the village, but she was afraid of taking on a path she didn't know so close to sunset for fear of getting caught out in the woods after dark. That left the hike up to the lookout point where they had launched the Christmas star, or the longer route around the back of the village which would eventually circle back to Comfort Cottage.

Even though there were only intermittent street lights and it might take longer than she expected, she would at least be on a proper road, so she opted for the latter choice.

Her decision had nothing to do with it passing the reindeer farm, where Henry might be working.

Nothing at all.

She started off confidently, but twenty minutes of hard walking later, she was within one bend of the farm, and was beginning to think about turning back. It would take about the same length of time to walk back down to the village, through the square, and up the road to her cottage as it would to complete the circle around past Simon's place … wouldn't it?

She stopped, shaking her head. She felt like a bit if a chancer, walking past Henry's at this time of day. Not even a chancer, more of a stalker.

'Don't be silly, Maggie,' she scolded herself, but the feeling persisted like a frustrating rain shower.

And what if Henry was there, what if he invited her in? What if she allowed him to apologise for not showing up to their not-really-a-date and something happened between them?

What if she was really happy about it, and then Dirk showed up tomorrow on the five o'clock train with a ring in his pocket?

With a frustrated scowl, she kicked at a drift of snow, expecting it to puff everywhere.

Instead, she kicked a buried rock.

She slipped, landing hard on her bum. Pain bloomed out from her ankle, and she knew immediately that she was hopping back to town.

She was trying to squeeze off a boot which had seemed to shrink with the cold when something howled out in the forest.

'Oh, please be a husky,' she whispered, wondering if wolves could smell fear. She was sure she remembered hearing about it on a TV documentary, but if so, how far away they could smell it from?

She managed to finally pull her boot free and gently massaged her foot. She had struck the rock on the outer side, twisting her foot inward and hurting her ankle. Brushing away the snow to reveal the culprit—a square block of granite with carvings on the side indicating it was probably an old mile-marker—she felt lucky she hadn't struck it straight on, or she might have broken her foot. As it was, she was likely out of tonight's dancing event.

After a couple of minutes of frantic rubbing it began to feel a little better, but when she tried to stand, she could only hobble a few steps before needing to sit down again in the snow.

She looked around her. Despite being no more than a mile from the village, she felt in the middle of nowhere. It was cold, and it was getting dark. Soon she would be crawling through dark spaces between the few street lights like something that had stumbled from the forest.

This wasn't the way it was supposed to be.

She shifted, trying to get up again, and felt the box containing the chocolate log bump against her back. She smiled grimly. At least she had food.

'Help!' she shouted. 'Help me!'

Her own voice echoed back from the trees. It was hopeless. She had no choice but to try to crawl for help.

The shadows were lengthening beneath the trees, and the fluffy snow was taking on an icy crust. She would freeze to death for sure.

A light blinked on through the trees. No more than a hundred metres away, Maggie was sure it hadn't been there a moment before.

Then she realised. It was a remote-sensor light, triggered by the onset of dusk.

But was it a street light, or a house?

She crawled across the road, hoping to get a better look around the curve. Her ankle throbbed with every movement, but eventually she made it, and saw to her horror that she was barely a stone's throw from the reindeer farm, Henry's cottage having been hidden by a stand of trees. The light blinked from outside his front door.

Maggie grimaced. Unless she wanted to stagger off into the forest to die, she had no choice but to crawl up to Henry's door and beg for help.

She tried to think of something interesting or witty to say, but could think of nothing, so she scraped and staggered her way onward until she had reached the little fence outside his cottage. Here she paused a moment to get her breath back, before crawling the last few metres up his path to his front door.

From inside came the lilting sound of a classical guitar recording of the concert from the night before. At least he had a pleasant taste in music. Exhausted, she tried to reach up and crack the door knocker, but she missed it completely and slumped against the door, hitting both elbows and her forehead.

The music cut off and footsteps came from inside. Maggie, suddenly panicking, tried to turn and crawl away, but her bad foot had got caught in an umbrella stand which now fell across her as the door opened to reveal Henry standing there.

'Oh, hello,' he said, frowning, then giving her a confused smile. 'I thought a bird had just slammed into the door.'

'No, no, not a bird,' Maggie said, her voice unnaturally high. 'I just came by to tell you I'm not angry that you didn't show up last night.' She pulled the crushed cardboard box she had dragged with her out from under her leg. 'And I brought you some chocolate log.'

18

RECOVERY

'RICE,' HENRY SAID AGAIN, SMILING HIS KIND SMILE AS he pressed the pack of frozen peas wrapped in a dishcloth against the bruise on Maggie's ankle while pressing a soft but strong palm against the other side. He pressed tightly, then relaxed his grip, then pressed tightly again, repeating over and over. 'Rest, ice, compression, elevation. The best way to treat sprains or impact injuries.'

Maggie smiled. 'Am I fixed yet?'

'Cinderella, you shall go to the ball. Just not the one tonight, if you know what's good for you.'

'Is that a dig on my clothing? It's not usually covered with dirt and snow, you know.'

'Oh, I like your clothing.' He patted his knee. 'My jeans are from Next too. There's one in Inverness. I might live here, but I do venture outside the village from time to time. Just to remind myself there's a world outside.'

'How did you know my clothes are from Next?'

'The label.'

'Oh.'

Maggie was unsure whether it was a good thing or not that she'd bought all her clothes with a staff discount. She'd never thought about it before.

'You tripped over a rock, you say?' Henry said, continuing his steady press and release. Despite her foot being raised over the edge of Henry's sofa, she didn't feel as awkward or compromised as she might with another near-stranger. Henry went about his work as methodically as a doctor on a home visit. She had watched his eyes for any sign he was trying to look farther up her leg, but so far he had been frustratingly chivalrous.

Maggie blushed. 'It was next to the verge.'

'You were walking along the verge?'

'Kind of.'

'You must have been walking pretty fast. This kind of bruise is reminiscent of a pretty solid knock. More like a, um, kick.'

Maggie's cheeks were so red she could have polished them and sold them in a fruit store. 'It was getting dark, you know. Where did you learn all this stuff, anyway? Mountaineering school?'

Henry smiled. 'Veterinary college. Animals get sprains too. Most often from kicking other animals or tripping over uneven terrain.'

'You're a vet?' Maggie wished there was a bucket of sand around she could pour over her head. 'I mean, Simon said you were, but I didn't think he meant an actually qualified one.'

'More like an amateur?' Henry laughed as Maggie continued to squirm. 'Oh, not anymore. Only for my reindeer and animals around the village. But yeah, five years in college at St Andrews, plus another five as a resident in a town just outside Edinburgh.'

'St Andrews? Isn't that where Prince—'

Henry laughed. 'Yeah. I don't recall seeing him on campus, and he's a couple of years older, but he might have been around there somewhere.'

'I'm sorry, I feel like an idiot.'

'Why?'

'Because—' Maggie wanted to wring her hands. There were too many reasons to put into words. 'I can't explain why. Not in less than fifteen minutes.'

Henry shrugged. 'I have plenty of time. I don't really watch television, bar the odd mini-series or documentary. I'd much rather hear you talk about why you're not an idiot, though.'

'I'm not an idiot?'

'Why would you be? You found your way here. Not many people do, but those that do always have an interesting story to tell.'

'I don't have any interesting stories. I'm just Maggie Coates, a thirty-two-year-old shop assistant from Cambridge who probably isn't going to get engaged this Christmas.'

Henry tilted his head. His eyes briefly met hers, then they returned their focus to her ankle. 'What makes you think not?'

'Because my boyfriend was supposed to show up

today, but put it off until tomorrow because of some stupid business meeting, except he didn't even tell me, and tomorrow is the last train so he might not show up at all—'

Henry patted her knee. Rather than being suggestive, it was frustratingly grandfatherly. 'Don't get so worked up,' he said. 'Keep your blood flow even. That's the quickest way to heal. I've got a feeling I can get you shipshape enough to make the dance floor on Christmas night. Until then you'll be taking it easy, though.'

'No more hiking?'

'No more unsupervised hiking, but if I put a splint into your boot you'll be able to get around. It's not as bad as it looks. You haven't torn anything. Just a twinge, really.'

Just a twinge. One that he was treating with far more care than any doctor might. Maggie blushed again. Was this a ploy to keep her in his cottage?

If it was, she wasn't against the idea, but that wasn't her style. Her boyfriend was coming tomorrow, and he was going to ask her to marry him, and—

'I need the loo,' she said, and then slapped a hand over her mouth so hard it made a cracking sound.

Henry smiled again. 'Sure. Do you think you can manage yourself? It'll be a good chance to test whether you can walk on your ankle or not. Don't move too quickly, though. If you knock it again it'll take longer to heal.'

He helped Maggie lower her leg to the floor then held her arm while she stood. She found herself taking longer than she perhaps needed just because she enjoyed the press of his fingers on her skin. He had such nice hands. Powerful and strong, yet gentle and soft. She could imagine them moving all over—

'Ouch!'

'Are you okay?'

She pressed harder on the floor. 'Yeah, it's not too bad. Just a little pain at first, but it feels a bit better now.'

'Can you walk on your own?'

'Um, no, I don't think so.'

You brazen hussy, she heard Renee's laughing voice say in her ear. *You totally can.*

Henry helped her across to the door, opening it for her with his free hand. Maggie hobbled across the hall to another door Henry indicated.

'The upstairs bathroom's a lot bigger, but I'm not sure you should be trying stairs right now.'

'Probably not a good idea.' She nodded at the door. 'I can probably make it from here.'

'Sure. I'll brew us some coffee. Plus, I fancy a piece of that chocolate log, if I can reconstruct it.'

She scowled at him until he grinned. With a gentle pat on her shoulder, he headed into the kitchen.

As she closed the door and gently lowered herself onto the loo, Maggie had a moment of clarity. She was shamelessly flirting, and allowing him to flirt back. She was still officially with Dirk, but she was coming dangerously close to cheating, something she had never done before. Even if Dirk was living up to Renee's favourite moniker, it wasn't right to play around behind his back.

Taking far longer than she needed, she listened to Henry moving about in the kitchen, the fizz of a kettle, the clinking of crockery. She needed to get out of here and back off; sure, he was handsome and kind, but she knew barely anything about him, and who was to say he didn't prey on every single woman with a broken heart who showed up each Christmas? He probably had more notches on his bedpost than she'd eaten calories since her arrival.

Just go for it, she heard Renee saying, a cheeky grin on her elvish face. *Why not? What have you got to lose? Just loosen up and have a good time.*

Maggie shook her head. No chance. While the idea of Henry and Dirk scuffling in the snow for her affection was quite appealing—she had no doubt Henry would win with little effort—it wasn't fair on either of them.

Plus, Dirk might not be perfect, but neither was Henry. He'd nearly run over her on a sleigh. He'd stood her up, even though they'd not really been on a date. He hadn't even apologised yet and had acted as though nothing had happened.

Perhaps if she could channel her anger about that, it would make it easier to get away before she really did do something to feel guilty about.

She climbed off the loo, struggling around on her bruised ankle, and went out into the hall.

The doors were all closed, and for a moment Maggie struggled to remember which was the door for the living room. Was it directly opposite, or just off to the left?

She tried the one to the left, but it opened onto a

study room. A desk was set up in a corner, a leather-bound journal open on top, a pen beside it. Rows of books stood on shelves. Glancing at some of the titles, Maggie saw books on veterinary practices, as well as poetry, literally classics, non-fiction history books, and numerous others that marked Henry as a closet intellectual rather than the boorish farmer she had first suspected.

But it was the object next to the chair that made her raise her eyebrows the most.

A classical guitar on a stand.

The door clicked behind her. Maggie dived out of the study, wincing as her bad ankle took the weight. Henry was watching her with a bemused smile.

'Sorry, wrong door,' she said.

'It's easy to get confused in a new place,' he said. 'I made coffee.'

Maggie couldn't let go of a sudden revelation. 'You were there, weren't you?' she said, pointing to the guitar. 'The snowman. It was you.'

For the first time, Henry looked off guard. He looked away, his own cheeks reddening.

'They didn't tell me I had to wear the suit,' he said.

19

RETURN

'IT'S A CORDOBA C10,' HENRY SAID, HOLDING THE guitar as gently as he might a new-born lamb. 'Handmade. It cost a small fortune. I bought it in Vilnius, the capital of Lithuania, believe it or not. I was nineteen years old, backpacking around Europe during the summer. I always liked to stay off the beaten track, so I found myself wandering out to this old part of town, and I found this little music shop having a closing sale.' He shrugged. 'It was the only item not discounted. The owner said he'd rather keep it himself than give it away cheap.'

Maggie nodded. She knew nothing about guitars other than that her father had owned a beat-up acoustic which he brought out once a year to slaughter *Happy Birthday* in front of her shocked school friends. 'It's beautiful,' she said. 'How did you afford it?'

Henry grinned. 'I was a gritty backpacker but I had a student credit card. Took a while to pay back, but it was worth it. Even then, the guy made me prove I could play it. Said he wouldn't sell it to a faker.'

He turned it over in his hands and delicately picked the first notes of *Walking in the Air*. Up close, the sound was like soothing fingers massaging into Maggie's neck. She closed her eyes. When she opened them again, Henry was grinning.

'Where did you learn to play like that?'

Henry shrugged. 'It's amazing how much time you have when you don't spend half of it on social media,' he said. 'Growing up in Hollydell we didn't have luxuries like the internet or Channel 5.'

'You do know that it's not cool to play classical guitar?' Maggie said with a grin. 'The kids that did it at school were all geeks.'

'What makes you think I'm not a geek?' Henry laughed, putting the guitar back on its stand. 'At school I was practically the president of the geek club. I can name thirteen different varieties of snail.'

'Because you're so—'

Don't say handsome. Maggie grimaced.

Say handsome! chirped Renee's voice.

'So, um, normal,' she muttered, then rubbed her forehead to hide another blush.

'Thanks, I think. Come on, the coffee's getting cold. And that monstrosity of a cake you made … well, I restored it as best I could, but it could fall apart at any moment. Tasted good, though. It wouldn't be safe for you to take it home, so I'm afraid you're going to have to leave it here.'

He helped her back into the living room and onto

the sofa, propping her leg up on a pillow again. She took an offered cup of coffee, which tasted perfectly brewed and sweetened with what was likely brown sugar. *What man buys brown sugar?* she wondered. *Is this an elaborate set-up?*

'What do you think of Hollydell?' Henry asked.

Maggie smiled. 'It's perfect.'

'Not too remote? A lot of people love the Christmas season, but couldn't handle it all year round.'

'You came back, though, didn't you? I mean, you said you were a vet near Edinburgh, but you're now here.'

Henry looked away for a moment, and Maggie sensed she had found a chink in his armour. If there was a secret there, it was best to leave it buried.

'I needed to come home,' he said at last. 'My mother always encouraged me to see the world, but she said one day I'd understand that the most perfect place in the world was the one you call home. Hollydell is my home. I run the reindeer farm, and help out around the village. I've never been happier.'

'Why don't—' Maggie began, but Henry laughed and put up a hand.

'How about you stop asking me the questions, and start answering some of mine? What's a beautiful girl like you doing in a place like Hollydell all on your own?'

'I'm not … are you putting a line on me? I'm not that kind of girl.'

Henry shrugged. 'I could tell you weren't from the first time you berated me. I think you're a little headstrong, but only when you're nervous. And I think you lack a little confidence in yourself.'

'I thought you were a vet, not a psychiatrist.'

'I just think it saves time to say what I think straight out. For what it's worth, I don't know what your boyfriend is playing at. The guy must be out of his mind.'

He held her gaze for a few seconds longer than was acceptable, until Maggie shifted on the sofa and felt a sharp bolt of pain race up her leg.

'Ouch,' she muttered.

Henry stood up. 'I should be getting you home,' he said. 'It's nearly seven o'clock.'

Maggie was stunned as she looked at the time. It had flown past. What was it Einstein had said about relativity? That a moment with your finger on a hot plate could feel like an hour, but an hour with a pretty girl could feel like a moment? *I bet Henry knows,* she thought.

'I'm not sure I can walk,' she said.

'Not a problem. I'll drop you back on the sleigh. I have to take George out for a turn around the village. Did you eat yet? I can cook you up something if you like.'

'Oh, it's no problem,' Maggie said, afraid that dinner was too much like a date and more than her conscience could handle. 'I have food at the cottage.'

As Henry nodded, Maggie tried to remember if she had anything other than hot chocolate and complimentary coffee, and whether her ankle could handle a hobble down to Barney's later.

'If you just wait here a while, I'll go saddle up the sleigh. I need to check the field and bring in the deer for the night. Give me about twenty minutes. Feel free to take a look around if you feel up to it.'

'Thanks.'

As he headed out, in truth Maggie was thankful just for a few minutes alone to make sense of her thoughts. Her emotions felt like a box of marbles thrown into a gushing river. Nothing made any sense. She needed to speak to Renee.

Barely any time seemed to have passed when she heard Henry come back in. He opened the door, smiled, and told her they were ready to go. Then he helped her to the door and assisted her to get her boots back on. The pain in her ankle had subsided enough that she felt capable of walking on it, but dancing or any type of strenuous activity was still out of the question.

Up close, the reindeer was a beautiful animal. Snorting as it shook its antlers, Henry smiled fondly and patted it on the back.

'George is the newest recruit for this year's Christmas night,' he said. 'I've just got to give her a bit more practice.'

'George?'

'Georgina. All Santa's reindeer are girls, didn't you know?'

Maggie shook her head. 'Um, no…?'

'Only females keep their antlers through winter,' Henry said. 'The males' grow back in spring.'

'What about Rudolph?'

Henry laughed. 'Rudolph isn't real.'

'Oh, and I guess the others are?'

Henry winked. 'You'll have to wait until Christmas night.'

Again, Maggie was reminded of the shape under the grey sheet in Simon's shed. She had written it off as part of a grand finale on Christmas night, some Santa Claus parade that would light up the village. Now, though, seeing the twinkle in Henry's eye, she wasn't so sure. Hollydell had shown her its magic often enough already.

Why not a little more?

After a bumpy ride through near darkness, Henry brought the sleigh to a stop outside Comfort Cottage and tied George to a fence post. Then, taking the same care he had before, he helped Maggie down the path to her door.

'Well, thank you for a lovely evening,' she said. 'I'm sorry for collapsing against your door.'

Henry shrugged. 'It needed another coat of paint. Those desperate scratches of yours will be gone in no time.'

As I will be too, she wanted to say, but couldn't bring herself. She smiled at Henry then went inside. Henry gave her a little wave before closing the door.

Hobbling around to the living room window that looked out onto the road took more effort than Maggie had expected with her bruised ankle. She made it to the drawn curtain and lifted up a corner just in time to see Henry climb onto the sleigh. George let out a snort. Henry cracked the reins and the sleigh started off.

At the last moment before he was gone from sight, he turned in the seat and gave the briefest of looks back.

Maggie ducked away from the window so hard she lost her balance and landed in a heap on the floor. Her foot struck the base of a bookcase and pain rattled up her leg. As she sat cross-legged and massaging it, all she could think about were those kind eyes, as they had briefly met hers.

20

REVELATION

SHE DIDN'T CALL RENEE RIGHT AWAY. HER MIND WAS filled with too much confusion, too great a jumble of thoughts and emotions to trust herself. First of all, she had to figure out what was going on.

Nothing had happened.

Henry had helped her out, but she couldn't deny how attracted she felt to the kindly vet-turned-reindeer farmer who also adopted stray cats and could possibly be the son of Santa Claus. However, he hadn't made a play on her—okay, he had called her beautiful, but in a matter-of-fact way that could be disregarded as a casual remark—and, in fact, had seemed quite keen to get her home, when letting her stay over might have been possible considering her condition.

Perhaps he had a wife or a girlfriend who had been due home? What if she lived in Inverness and was due to visit him for Christmas? After all, there weren't a lot of jobs around Hollydell.

Maggie squeezed her temples, shaking her head. Perhaps she shouldn't wait for Dirk to show or not show, but should get down the station tomorrow and get on the train for herself. What was supposed to be a romantic holiday with her long-term boyfriend had turned into a spaghetti junction of uncertainty.

Barney's, she discovered from her guidebook, did a delivery service. She made a call to the restaurant, explained her situation, and ordered a small pizza to be delivered. The man told her twenty minutes.

She set herself a place at the table, put a Christmas CD she found in a rack on the hi-fi player in the corner, and set her table—a knife and fork and a glass of red wine.

Everything would be fine; all she had to do was wait it out.

The phone rang.

Maggie stared at it, wondering who could possibly know the number. Was it Renee, or Dirk? She had called both from the phone. Or was it Henry, checking in on her to make sure she was all right?

She sighed. Most likely it was Barney's checking on her order.

She picked it up.

'Mags?'

'Renee.' Maggie let out a long sigh. 'I'm so glad you called. I was just thinking to call you. You see, something happened. That guy I told you about, I hurt my ankle and he patched me up. We had coffee and it turns out he didn't stand me up, but he was dressed as a snowman—'

'I don't think Dirk's coming.'

There was something so flat about Renee's tone that it severed Maggie's rambling like a hot knife.

'Ren?'

'I tried to get through on your mobile earlier but it kept going to voicemail. And honestly, Mags, I wasn't sure what to say.'

'Ren, what's going on?'

'I had the afternoon off,' Renee said. 'I fancied a quick trip down to London for a bit of last minute Chrimbo shopping. You know, as you do. Always something you've forgotten, right?'

'Yeah, and?'

'Well, I remembered you telling me where Dirk worked, and I was playing about on Google Maps, you know, wasting time on the train, and I realised it wasn't that far from the station, so I thought I might see if I could bump into him after he left work and find out what the monkeys he's been playing at, messing you around like that.'

'You went to where he worked?'

'Well, not exactly. I went to the industrial park where his company is and found a pub right across from the main entrance. I got myself a vodka and tonic and a portion of chips and waited for him to come out, figuring it would be around five. Mags, honestly, I only wanted to give him a verbal slap for the way he's been treating you.'

'Thanks, Ren. I can always count on you.'

'And then … and then ….'

'Come on, Ren, this is like waiting for a Christmas present I really don't want. Just tell me.'

'It was nearly half five and the train was due at six so I was packing up to go. I figured he was being all high management and that and staying late so I'd miss my chance. Then I saw him.'

'You saw Dirk?'

'He was all glammed up in one of those long, black exec jackets. He looked like he'd been pumped out of an office worker production line, all sleek and manicured. I hardly recognised him. Even his hair was all slapped over and greased down.'

'Yeah, okay, so he looked like a director—'

A sharp sob came from the other end of the line.

'Ren, what is it?'

'He was … with someone.'

Even as Maggie said, 'What, like a colleague or someone?' she knew she was wrong.

'With a woman. A girl, more like. She can't have been more than twenty-five.' Renee was sobbing on the other end of the line, and it took a few seconds for her to calm down long enough to continue. 'She was like a proper office tart. Tiny skirt that ought to get her arrested. So much makeup you could have peeled it off her face and sold it in one of those art shops that does the Venetian masks. And a good job too, because, no offense to her, but she was a right moose, Mags. She was like a frog next to you. I know you're always pretending that you're not pretty but you're totally gorgeous, and this girl, honestly….'

'Oh.' A lump had appeared in Maggie's throat,

making it difficult to form words. She just nodded over and over, as though Renee were sitting in the room with her. 'Oh. So … are you sure … are you sure they weren't just friends?'

'He was holding her arm. They came right into the pub, right in front of me. He didn't even notice me standing there with my jaw on the floor. They went up to the bar, and his hand was all over her back. I mean, it would have been romantic if it had been you, even though he's a jerk, but it wasn't you. And they ordered two glasses of white wine and they turned around and clinked them together. And Dirk said something like, "Merry Christmas, darling." I wanted to be sick. So I just held up my phone and said, "Merry Christmas, jerk," and took a picture.'

Maggie stared. 'You got a picture?'

'I'll send it to your phone if you like. I didn't want to just fire it off if you're out of reception, because it might just vanish, or show up at a really bad time, or I—I don't know. I'm rambling now, Mags. Oh, I'm so sorry. It's Christmas, and I know you're waiting for him, and while I've always thought you could do way better, I just wanted you to be happy….'

Renee started crying again. Maggie felt hollow inside. She rested the phone on her lap and just stared ahead, seeing through the walls of Comfort Cottage, out into the snow of Hollydell, over the hills and across the fields, right back to Cambridge where her hopes and dreams of getting married had finally died an ugly death.

'He's not coming,' she muttered. 'He's found someone else.'

'Mags, you still there?'

She lifted the phone. 'Ren? Yeah, sorry. It's just a bit of a shock, that's all. Did he say anything to you?'

She heard Renee blow her nose. Despite everything, she smiled.

'He just said, "Oh, Renee, it's not what it looks like," but it was totally what it looked like, you know?'

'Perhaps they were just friends. You know, it's Christmas; people are a lot friendlier with each other. Maybe they'd just done a deal or something, I don't know.'

She was clutching at straws, but she couldn't help it. They'd been together so long, and for Dirk to cheat on her like this, on the eve of Christmas … she didn't want to believe it.

'Mags, I would totally be with you there, but the tart, she turned to him and said, "Oh, Dirk"—but she pronounced it that posh way, that makes it sound like "Dahk"—"Oh, Dahk, is this her? Is this your ex? What's she doing here?" I might have got a couple of those words wrong, but she clearly said "ex". I heard that as clearly as I'm hearing you now.'

'And what did he say?'

'I don't know, because I ran out. I wanted to stand there and berate him, but there was a limited train service on and it was the next train or get back at midnight. I'm so sorry, Mags. I cried the whole way home. He's such a jerk. He couldn't even just tell you, and he's let you go up there to Scotland on your own. Oh, he's suck a *jerk*.'

The doorbell went. Maggie almost fell off the edge of the phone table.

'Hang on a minute. Pizza's here.'

'You're in getting pizza? Shouldn't you be out ice-skating or something?'

'I told you, I hurt my ankle. Wait a minute.'

She hobbled to the door, and opened it to find Andrew standing there in a cap, holding out a box with a pizza decorated with little Christmas trees on the top. 'Delivery,' he said. 'I heard from Henry that you'd hurt your foot. Are you all right?'

Maggie smiled, swallowing down her emotions. 'It's feeling much better,' she said.

Andrew nodded. 'That's good. I hope to see you around the village tomorrow. If need anything at all, call my mother at the village hall or just give us a call at Barney's.'

'Thank you.'

'Goodnight.'

She closed the door and went back to the phone table. 'Ren, you still there?'

'Took you a while to get that pizza.'

'That was the brother of the guy I was telling you about.'

'He has a brother?'

'Yeah, he drives the train.'

'And delivers pizzas?'

'And the post, and a few other things. They seem to be pretty good at multi-tasking up here.'

'Sounds like a pretty interesting place.'

'It is.'

Renee was quiet a moment. 'I'm sorry, Mags. I didn't want to tell you, but I'm your friend, and something like this … I know it's nearly Christmas, but I couldn't keep it from you. Maybe I was mistaken; maybe it was all a misunderstanding. He didn't call her "darling", she didn't refer to you as his ex, they weren't all touchy with each other … maybe I'm just going insane in my own spinsterhood? Anyway, I have to finish preparing the song sheets for tomorrow's carol singing at the shelter. That's what taking the afternoon off has done for me. And ruined your life. So sorry, Mags.'

'You're the best, Ren. Friends forever?'

'Of course. And you know, you're a free agent now. You can totally go for that hot reindeer farmer. He is hot, isn't he?'

Maggie forced a laugh. She remembered Henry's kind eyes, his strong hands. 'Oh, he's a total dish,' she said, but as they said their goodbyes and Maggie hung up, she couldn't feel anything for Henry. In fact, she couldn't feel anything at all.

21

BLAME GAME

Maggie woke up on the sofa with a sore head. The bottle of wine she had opened for her chat with Renee was empty, and half a congealed pizza was stinking out the room. She rolled onto the floor and stood up, wincing at the pain in her ankle, but her foot could at least take her weight.

It was a little after eight a.m. She opened a window, letting in a cold draft, which immediately made her feel better, clearing out the smell. Outside, snow was falling heavily, and the line of fairy lights along her front fence was glowing through a fresh deposit.

December 23rd. Dirk would be here today.

No, he wouldn't.

The recollection of her conversation with Renee hit her like a charging moose. She staggered back to the sofa and slumped down, wrapped in a chill that was slowly stripping away the layers of her hangover but revealing the mess of her love life at the same time.

Dirk had someone else. They were never going to get married.

She sat up straight. But what if he still showed up?

Dirk knew Renee; they'd hung out on several occasions, even though she thought he was a jerk and he thought she was an airhead. He'd often told Maggie how he felt jealous of their closeness, so surely he would know Renee would reveal what she had seen. But would he still show up to try to brush it away, get a last bit of action before canning Maggie in the New Year?

She lifted her damaged foot onto her knee and gave it a prod and a wiggle. Her ankle had a black ring around it, but it didn't hurt too much. It was a little stiff, but Henry's medical expertise had fixed her up pretty good. She felt sure she could walk on it, and with her boot acting as a de facto splint, she could probably get around the village without too much trouble.

She got up and went and did what needed to be done—swallowed a couple of aspirin from a packet she always kept in her bag, used the loo and took a shower, put on enough makeup to stop people running from her screaming if they saw her hobbling out of a snowstorm —then she struggled to the door and put on her coat and boots.

She thought about trying the phone, but Dirk wouldn't answer. He probably wouldn't listen if she left him a voicemail. Unless he knew it was her, he would likely ignore the call completely.

The snow was falling pretty heavily. It took a long time to get down to the train station, but Maggie went slowly, careful not to twist her ankle any more, but she found that after a bit of walking it felt a lot better.

The station was deserted, the train sitting at its buffers snug beneath a blanket of fresh snow. No prints led to or from the entrance. She was alone on the platform where she took up her regular seat near the end.

She took out her phone. Probably due to the snow, the reception was poor, but she had a couple of bars. She had, as usual, forgotten to charge it, but there was enough battery left to send a few messages or make a short call.

Taking a deep breath, she found DIRK in her recent call list and pressed CALL. It went through to voicemail, but she decided not to leave a message. She couldn't trust what she would say. She didn't feel angry—after all, the last few weeks of sparse contact had done its homework, setting her up for this—but she didn't want to sound too apologetic either. Maybe she wasn't good enough for him anymore, but she couldn't help that. She was Maggie Coates, and if that wasn't enough for Dirk-who-pronounced-it-D-ah-k, she couldn't do anything about it.

She opened up her messages and began typing.

I talked to Renee. I wanted to wish a Merry Christmas to you and your new girlfriend. You should have just told me. We were together for four years, Dirk. I'm sorry you couldn't just tell me it was over.

She frowned at the use of the word 'sorry', but it wasn't a direct apology, so she let it ride. With an angry scowl, she pressed SEND.

The snow was starting to ease. From somewhere out on the road she heard an engine, so she got up to have a look. Andrew was driving a small snow-plough, slowly clearing the roads. She watched him do a circuit of the square outside the station then head back up the road to the village, two furrows of churned snow left in his wake.

Her phone pinged.

She opened it too quickly, dropping it on the ground. Luckily the case took the impact, but she took a deep breath before she scooped it up.

Dirk.

Pretty Pea ... it wasn't how I wanted you to find out. I was planning to come up today, I promise. I just got overloaded with work. Claire was there to help me out when I needed it. It wasn't planned, you understand, don't you, Pretty Pea? I've just not felt much affection from you in the last few weeks—

Maggie howled with rage and threw the phone away with as much strength as she could muster. It struck the wall of the opposite platform and exploded into bits of metal, glass and plastic.

As her rage-filled scream died away, the only sounds came from the soft patter of snowflakes falling on the train tracks, the thump of Maggie's beating heart, and the distant growl of the snow-plough's engine.

'Oops,' she said aloud, grimacing.

She hadn't finished reading the message, but she had read enough. He had actually tried to blame her, as though it had been her and not him who had been distant, putting their relationship at arm's length.

Renee was right.

As her anger faded, the fact that she had just smashed her smartphone became reality. It was her sacred possession, protected like a child or a dear pet, and now it lay in bits on the opposite platform. She hadn't realised she could get so much power into a throw.

The doubts came rushing in like a troupe of dancers from the side of a stage, encircling her, whispering and insinuating, clouding her judgment. Perhaps Dirk's message had gone on to apologise, to say he'd made a mistake, that he was coming anyway, that he was hoping to patch things up?

Now she would never know.

And the freedom of it felt increasingly welcome as the seconds ticked by.

'I'm single,' she said, her voice echoing back at her from under the platform's overhanging roof. 'I'm single again, after four years.' Then, as though to balance herself out, she added, 'I've just been dumped.'

Unsure which line of thought she should follow, she curled up on the bench, her head held tightly in her hands.

22

FRIENDLY ADVICE

It appeared the other platform was no longer used and had no stairway access, so it took Maggie an awkward few minutes to climb down on to the tracks, wade through the snow and climb up the other side. There though, keen not to be seen as a litterer as well as a Billy No Mates and a single thirty-something who'd just been dumped on the eve of Christmas, she retrieved the pieces of her smartphone and put them into a bin at the end of the platform.

Despite the initial shock of her phone's wanton destruction, Maggie still remembered life before mobile phones took over the world, and knew she'd get used to being without it. It also meant she wouldn't need to keep walking down to the station in the hunt for the odd bar or two of reception. In some ways, she felt liberated. No more social media to check. No more staring at a static screen waiting for it to illuminate with an incoming message. On the other hand, she wouldn't know if someone was trying to contact her urgently. As she walked out of the exit into the little plaza with its Christmas tree almost buried in snow, she wondered if she was emerging as a new woman, or as a broken version of the old one.

One thing was for sure, the life she had become used to was over. Four years, and until the last few months, they'd been happy. They'd talked of moving in together, of one day having children, of getting married.

Or had it been her talking about that stuff?

As she tried to recall their conversations, she couldn't remember whether they had been one way, or mutual. Had she been laying down all the future plans while he just nodded along, or had he been a willing participant? Had his move to London and his affair been an unfortunate circumstance or had he planned an escape all along?

The doubts tugging on her at least helped to mask the ongoing ache in her ankle. She stared at the road leading up to Hollydell, the space Andrew had cleared already dusted over with fresh snow, and took deep breath.

Her new life began now.

Halfway across the plaza, she saw someone on skis coming down the other way, gliding through the fresh snow along the verge. The figure stopped. Hands rose to lift goggles, and Emma smiled at Maggie, then cocked her head and frowned.

'What are you doing down here?'

In her mind, a thousand answers clamoured for attention. *I was just going ice fishing. I saw a bear and was aiming to wrestle it with my bare hands. I was planning to hotwire the train and take it for a spin to Inverness and back.*

But the one that rose above all the others was the least wanted: 'I just got dumped,' she sobbed, bursting into a flood of tears.

~

'Drink it,' Emma said, holding up the glass. 'Pinch your nose if you have to. Get it down your gut and we can start the rebuilding process.'

'I hate brandy,' Maggie said.

'No, you love it. You just haven't figured it out yet. Come on, girl. It's a Christmas spice edition. It tastes just like a mince pie.'

Maggie chugged back the glass, then coughed into her hand.

'Just a little stronger,' Emma said, patting her on the back.

The Lodge, Maggie was just finding out, was the closest thing Hollydell had to a nightclub. A smart restaurant styled like a German beer hall, it was set just back into the forest along the road past the park. Almost out of sight of the village, during the day it served cosmopolitan food, but as soon as nine p.m. ticked around, the tables were pushed to the side and a disco ball began to spin. Now, at just a little after ten a.m., its tables were scattered with couples and small groups tucking into continental breakfasts.

John and Ted, sitting at the adjacent table, had

crowded around to offer words of advice when Emma was stuck for something to say. Already feeling dizzy and cajoled by Emma, Maggie gave them a blow-by-blow account of what had happened with Dirk. As soon as she had concluded with the part about throwing her phone against the station wall, and just as she opened her mouth to explain what she thought were Dirk's reasons for going off with someone else, Emma lifted a hand.

'I know what's coming, and I won't allow it. You're not going to now rub yourself into the dirt with a mouthful of garbage about how everything was your fault. I've heard that too many times before. We don't need to meet this guy to know that your friend's assessment is probably spot on.'

'He changed,' Maggie said. 'We used to be so close, but after he went to London, he became a different person.'

'What's done is done,' Ted said. 'What we can't allow is for it to ruin the rest of your holiday. Emma has the right idea. Let's all get drunk and then go play snow angel.'

'Snow angel?'

John, a few years younger than Ted but with robin-red cheeks and thick glasses, grinned. 'Oh, yes. Fresh snow like today is just perfect.'

'You stand under a tree and shake it,' Ted said. 'And you become a snow angel.'

'That sounds ace!' Emma shouted, banging her coffee cup on the table top. 'Let's all do some shots and then head out. There's that big fir tree up by the turn down to the Lodge; do you think we could shift it if we all try together?'

'Worth a go,' John said. 'Although I think you and I will have to do the heavy lifting. Maggie here's got a kooky ankle and Ted's got the stick.'

Ted patted John's shoulder. 'I can play snow angel with the best of them,' he wheezed. 'But what about a more long-term fix for young Maggie here? She's had her heart broken.'

'It's obvious, isn't it?' Emma said. 'You worship at the altar of the single life. You dedicate your life to never allowing another man to encroach on it again.'

'They're not all bad,' John said. 'Ted's all right.'

'Just all right?'

'Well, you know, he can cook.'

'What are you trying to say?'

Emma laughed. She patted Maggie on the thigh hard enough to make Maggie wince. 'Look. Nothing but trouble. I'll teach you how to Nordic ski after lunch.'

'I'll probably be too drunk at this rate. And it's hard enough to walk as it is.'

'She can come with us,' John said. 'Ellie's running a cooking class after lunch. Marshmallow making.'

'I thought marshmallows only came in packets?' Emma said.

'So did we,' John answered. 'That's why we signed up.'

'Sounds good,' Maggie said. 'I can put them in my brandy.' Then, as though the idea of something so frivolously joyful was undeserved, she burst into tears.

'What are we going to do with her?' John said,

patting her on the back as Emma wiped her face with a warm cloth, two gestures that, while unnecessary, felt strangely comforting.

Ted laughed. 'I don't think we need to do a thing. Let Hollydell spin its magic web. Perhaps there's someone else out there for her. Perhaps he's even right here.'

'What about Andrew?' Emma said. 'Ellie's always prattling on about getting him married off. He's just far too content driving the train and working around the village, she always says. Like he's married to Hollydell.'

'I don't like beards,' Maggie sobbed. 'They're itchy.'

John and Ted exchanged a glance. 'Well, what about his brother?' John said.

'Henry is rather fetching,' Ted added.

Emma shook her head. 'Absolutely not. He's obviously gay.'

'Why?'

'No straight man could ever be that cultured. He's a qualified vet, which is about as educated as you can get. He's well-travelled. Musical. He writes poetry—'

'He writes poetry?' Maggie said.

'Oh, yes,' John said. 'Last year he and Andrew put on an exhibition in the village hall. Andrew painted landscape scenes to go along with Henry's poetry. It was really quite wonderful.'

'Andrew paints?'

'Oh, yes. Quite a talented pair, those boys.'

'Just shows what you can achieve when you don't spend half your life on the internet,' Emma said, prompting laughter from John and Ted.

'Henry's gay?'

Emma shrugged. 'Well, in all the time we've all been coming here, no one's ever known him to have a girlfriend. He's always been up there on that farm, looking after his reindeer.'

Maggie frowned. There was much to suggest he had no interest in her. He had called her beautiful without seeming remotely embarrassed. How could he have possibly done that unless he was either a player or gay?

'You know what,' she said, sitting up suddenly, 'I think I know what the best thing to do is.' She lifted a fist. 'Enjoy myself. Come on, let's have another drink, then go play snow angel, then take a walk around the village to build up an appetite for lunch.'

Emma turned to John and Ted and nodded. 'The girl's back with us,' she said. 'That's the spirit.'

They all lifted their respective cups and clinked.

'To Christmas, and getting over break-ups,' Emma shouted.

Maggie smiled. 'To Christmas,' she said.

23

HOPES AND FEARS

Wading through the quagmire of her emotions and getting safely to the other side wasn't going to be easy for Maggie, but Emma, John and Ted were certainly doing their best to help.

With Emma hollering orders to John while Maggie gingerly tried to help and Ted leaned on his walking stick and laughed, they attempted to shake the large pine at the end of the path up to The Lodge hard enough to turn them all into snow angels. Perhaps two hundred years of sterling wood refused to even budge, but after ten minutes of making gleeful fools of themselves, a decent gust of wind passed their way and did a passable job.

With Emma holding on to Maggie and John holding on to Ted, they made their snow-covered way back down to the village.

Emma then excused herself to continue her Nordic skiing trek, so John and Ted took Maggie on a gentle walking tour of the village now the snow had eased. They pointed out several restaurants and shops she was yet to visit, told her what she could expect from each of the stalls lined up around the village square when they opened around six p.m.

Tonight's main event, they told her, was the grand opening of the Christmas Market, even though a few select food stalls had been opening for the last couple of days. Tonight would see the opening of the souvenir stalls that sold handmade toys in a variety of traditions based on old Arctic Circle techniques. There would be a concert where various groups would perform traditional dances and songs, a couple of short dramatic pieces and some solo musical pieces. Henry would be there, John told her with a wink, playing something on the classical guitar. Maggie just shrugged and said she'd check her diary.

Hollydell was laid out like a spider's web with the village hall its central eye. Leading her up one street through a tree-lined avenue, John and Ted pointed out the houses and workshops of several resident artisans, toymakers, artists, watchmakers, even a retired composer. Hollydell was a haven for those who didn't need to work proper jobs, John told her with a smirk. Every one of them added a little something to Hollydell's magic, and if you stayed after Christmas through New Year, many of them ran workshops and open houses where you could learn their various techniques. Ted claimed that he now knew more about wooden furniture than B&Q.

'I met one guy,' Maggie said. 'Simon, he said he was called. He seemed to be a carpenter.'

John and Ted exchanged glances. 'The best way to explain Simon is that he's the village's figurehead,' Ted said. 'As a result, you won't see him much. He's always there, but he's behind the scenes, if you know what I mean.'

'What Ted's trying to say is that we'll let you learn about Simon by yourself.'

'That sounds mysterious.'

'Well, I guess it is.'

Before she could answer, Ted tugged her sleeve. 'It's nearly noon. These old bones need sustenance.'

They took her down a winding lane to a quaint café called Santa's Cabin where they ordered a lunch set of brie and maple sandwiches. Maggie balked at the choice, but on her first bite found them to be mouth-wateringly delicious. She finished her round before John or Ted were halfway through theirs, and promptly ordered another.

'I'm comfort-eating,' she told their raised eyebrows. 'That's okay, isn't it?'

'We might have to do a bit of consolation-eating,' Ted said, giving her a wink. 'But, you know, they do this chocolate cake that last year I literally almost died for….'

'He fell off his chair,' John said. 'After his first bite. Luckily he didn't drop the cake.'

Maggie looked from one to the other, narrowing her eyes. 'Well, I need a lot of comfort,' she said.

An hour later, full to the point where walking hurt her stomach more than it hurt her ankle, she headed back to the village hall with John and Ted for marshmallow-making class.

Ellie was preparing in the kitchens with a couple of familiar faces—Gail from catering, Phillip from the delicatessen—who would be leading the class, he announced at the beginning—and Linda's husband Len. Linda herself had gone on another dog-sled tour.

When everyone was ready, Phillip gave them a short speech about the wonders of marshmallows. While during the day they would find him working behind the counter of his deli selling various cured meats and cheeses from around the world, over the next few days by night they would find him running one of the confectionary stalls around the village square. His specialty was homemade, vegetarian marshmallows.

Using agar-agar, a jelly-like substance produced from algae, in place of the animal-derived gelatine, he would show them how to make the best marshmallows they had ever tasted. Maggie's stomach grumbled as he read out the list of ingredients—most of which seemed to be sugar or something sugary—and she gave her waistline a guilty pat. Still, her ankle was feeling better, so a long walk before dinner would work all the forthcoming calories off … before she piled them on again at the Christmas market. With a shrug, she convinced herself that her comfort-eating excuse could carry her right through to the New Year, after which she could change her life if she really wanted. Wasn't that what new years were for?

Paired with Len—who laughed when she confessed that she didn't really work at Cambridge University as Linda assumed, but at a shop that had a bit of a view of a spire that might or might not be part of an old building that might or might not have some connection to the university—they worked up a delicious sugar storm.

Their mixtures, once poured into a tray, had to sit overnight. Phillip checked each effort, nodding with satisfaction, then asked everyone to come back the next morning. There would be a celebratory hot chocolate session, he told them, to a series of cheers.

It was nearly four o'clock when they came out of the village hall. Twilight was upon them, the sun long set behind the mountains. The village glowed like a Christmas card, lights twinkling everywhere.

Before they left, though, Ellie called them together to make an announcement.

'I just thought I'd let you know, we're expecting heavier snow than usual tomorrow morning and into the afternoon,' she said. 'Tomorrow is Christmas Eve, traditionally our busiest day of the year, and while we don't expect it to cause any cancellations to the planned events, we would like to ask you to take special care, especially if you go out on any of the trails. Our staff will be checking everywhere within the village's borders, but please don't leave any of the paths. Also, while we'll be doing our best to let all the guests know, feel free to pass this message on. Like I say, I'm sure it'll all pass without a hitch, but here in Hollydell—as I'm sure you've noticed—we get a lot more snow than the rest of Scotland.'

There were knowing nods all round, and a few smiles.

'Just be safe out there,' Ellie said. 'Tomorrow is Christmas Eve. Most of you know what kind of party we have, but for those of you who don't, you'll never forget it. We're hoping that this year is the best ever.'

The guests headed off to their respective cottages to relax for a while before the opening of the Christmas Market. Maggie said goodbye to John, Ted, and Len, then started up the road toward Comfort Cottage before abruptly coming to a halt halfway there.

If she headed down to the train station, she would make it just in time to greet the five o'clock train, the last one before Christmas.

Dirk wouldn't be on it. He couldn't be. But what if he was?

Maggie turned and started the long hobble downhill. While her ankle was feeling better, she'd rather neglected to rest it as she perhaps should have, so each step was accompanied by a dull ache.

By the time she made it, the clock outside the station was showing five to five. She climbed the steps to the platform and took her usual bench at the end. She stared across at the place where her phone had shattered and wondered if Dirk had sent her any apologetic messages. Perhaps worried about receiving no reply, he had decided to come anyway, just to make sure she was all right. There was a part of her that wanted to see him step down from the train, give her a pathetic smile and wrap her in his arms. It wasn't too late. If he said he was truly sorry, she would forgive him. It was Christmas after all, and everyone made mistakes.

Movement at the other end of the platform caught her eye. Maggie looked up to see Emma come up the steps, look one way then back, catch sight of Maggie and then come striding up the platform, shaking her head.

She was still wearing a ski helmet.

'What are you doing here? I saw you walk across the plaza. I thought we talked about this.'

Maggie rubbed her hands together, tears in her eyes.

'He might still come,' she said. 'He might.'

Emma sat down beside her and wrapped her in a bear hug that was uncomfortably tight. 'Oh, Maggie. When are you going to snap out of this? I've only known you a couple of days, but I can already tell you that this guy isn't worth a moment of your attention. You're one of the loveliest people I've ever met, and you're wasted on this clueless muppet. Honestly, if my hands weren't so cold they felt like blocks of ice, I'd slap some sense into you.'

'I just … I wanted so much … I thought we'd be together forever.'

Emma sighed. 'Life picks and chooses its moments to throw a spanner in the works. Obviously Christmas isn't the best time for a broken heart, but it's certainly the best time to start mending one. You know who I bumped into earlier?'

'Who?'

'Henry.'

'Henry?'

'He was out mending fence posts. With the snow, some of the reindeer get a little frisky and go wandering off to look for food. We talked about you.'

'You did? What did he say?'

'He said that he'd bumped into you. When I told him I'd seen you hobbling about, he told me he'd fixed you up. No, he didn't refer to you as a farm animal.'

'I didn't say—'

'I'm just making sure. He also said he'd given you a lift home. He mentioned that you were waiting for your boyfriend, and I'm afraid I went off on one. Obviously I've only heard about Dirk from you, but he sounds like a bit of a … well, whatever.'

'And what did Henry say?'

'Not a lot. He's not much of a talker, not like many of us.' Emma gave herself a pat on the cheek. 'I'm afraid that once I was done with my exposition, he simply said that he thought the guy was crazy. He said he'd have been waiting at the station for you.'

'Did he really say that?'

'Yes. Why would I lie?'

'I thought you said he was gay.'

Emma rolled her eyes. 'He should be gay. No man that cultured should ever be straight. But frankly, no one knows. He's certainly not a womaniser, unless he keeps the kind of secrets that would make a village this size implode. Don't you know anything about small towns? Everyone knows everything. Henry is as single as can be, so what better time than Christmas for a damsel in distress to come waltzing into his life?'

'I'm not a damsel in distress, and I'm not on the rebound, either. In fact, I'm quite enjoying being single.'

Farther down the line, the lights of the train appeared between two dark hills.

Emma sighed. 'Which is why you're sitting here at the end of the platform, in case your cheating boyfriend has the audacity to show up even after being rumbled?'

Maggie shrugged. 'I like the quiet.'

'Everywhere in Hollydell is quiet. Well, here's your moment of truth.'

The train came steaming into the station, slowing as it moved along the platform, its brakes squealing as it came to stop. It shuddered and let out a hiss of steam. The whistle blew once, then the cab door opened and Andrew climbed down. Maggie watched as he walked along the platform, opening the doors, welcoming the passengers as they stepped down. There were more than yesterday, but still only a couple of dozen.

And Dirk was not among them.

'Are we good?' Emma said.

Maggie let out a sigh. 'We're good. I'm heartbroken, but I can already feel the tug of the stitches. I'll live.'

Emma laughed. 'Oh, you've never really lived until you've seen the Christmas Market in full swing. Let's get going. We have just enough time for a couple of pick-me-ups before the grand opening.'

24

SECRET VISITOR

DESPITE EMMA'S INSISTENCE THAT THEY GET plastered before the start of the Christmas Market, Maggie insisted she needed a change of clothes, so she arranged to meet Emma later and hurried as best she could back to Comfort Cottage.

As always, as soon as she was alone the doubts crept in, but she had decided that in order to truly move forward in life she needed to face them. Dirk and her failed relationship was a gremlin on her shoulder that she needed to shrug off. And falling into Henry's arms— or anyone else's for that matter—was not the way to handle it. The best thing to do was follow Emma's lead: be single and proud, and make damn sure she had a wonderful Christmas.

It wouldn't hurt to call Renee first, though.

'Mags—hold on, I'm fixing a broken Christmas light with one hand while holding open an oven with the other.'

'How are you holding the phone?'

'Third hand.'

'Oh.'

'That's that. All good. Right. What happened?'

Maggie recounted the message from Dirk as best she could, following up with how she had smashed her phone.

'Girl power, good work. But you definitely didn't go down to the station just in case, did you?'

'Um….'

'You did.'

'Kind of, yeah. Just in case. He wasn't there.'

'He called me at the kid's home. No idea how he got the number or even knew I worked there, but I guess he has resources now he's a hotshot director. He wanted to know if I'd heard from you.'

'What did you tell him?'

'I told him he was an asshole. I told him you never wanted to see him again and that you hoped he had a rubbish Christmas.'

'Did you really?'

'And then I slammed the phone down on him. Well, I didn't actually slam it, but I put it down hard.'

'And he didn't call back?'

'No. But I looked him up on Facebook. You remember how he never had his status as "in a relationship" the whole time he was with you?'

'Yeah, he thought it was corny. It didn't bother me.'

'Well, he's using it now. She must be as hard as nails. He'll regret cheating on you, Mags. You're such a catch.'

'I don't feel like one.'

'That's what makes you one. You're pretty and nice, but you're also humble.'

'Yeah, okay, that's enough. I don't feel any of those things. In fact, all I feel at the moment are fat and sad.'

'Mags, you're in an awesome Christmas village filled with great food and dishy reindeer farmers. Now's the time to celebrate.'

'I don't feel much like it. I'm doing my best, but it's so easy to say, isn't it?'

Renee sighed. 'Yeah, it is. Will it help if I sing *We Wish You a Merry Christmas* down the phone?'

Maggie laughed. 'Probably not—'

A knock came on the door. Maggie looked up. The sound of footsteps crunching in the snow receded away.

'Hang on a minute. That's a bit creepy. Someone just played knock and run on me.'

'I'll stay on the line while you go and check. Don't worry, I'll get Inverness police station up on the speed dial just in case. Right ... hang on ... okay, you're good. Go and check.'

Maggie didn't feel particularly nervous, because the footsteps had been moving away, and she couldn't imagine a weirdo in Hollydell. She put down the phone and peered through the spyhole. There were the tracks, heavier, closer ones coming up to the door, then lighter, more spread out ones leading away.

Cautiously, she cracked the door. A light snow was falling, creating a veil over the streetlight outside her cottage. No one was there, and the street outside was deserted. She was about to go back inside, when she glanced down, and saw a wooden box sitting on the outside step.

'Oh.'

She picked the box up and went back inside, closing the door. She carried it with her to the phone table and set it down.

'Ren, someone left me something.'

'Well, don't keep me in suspense, open it up. I can't believe you even bothered to pick up the phone.'

'It's got a clasp on it. I think it's hand carved. It's really pretty, the kind of thing you'd get in an arts and craft shop but wouldn't actually use for anything.'

Maggie lifted the clasp and peered inside. Various items of food were arranged in an orderly fashion. She saw a couple of sandwiches, a plastic container of what looked like soup, several roast potatoes wrapped in a tissue. There was even a bottle of mineral water with two aspirin still in their plastic case taped to the side.

On top of everything was a card in an envelope.

When she described the contents to Renee, her friend squealed with excitement. 'Open it!'

Maggie ripped the envelope's edge and pulled out a pretty Christmas card. The picture on the front showed three reindeer grazing in a snowy field. Even without the view through the trees of a train line, Maggie would have guessed this was a print of a painting done by Andrew.

She smiled as she opened it and read the message aloud to Renee.

'I didn't know if you'd make it out tonight or not, but if you're housebound here's something to keep you alive. I'll come past tomorrow morning to check on you. Sorry I can't stop, but I have to get to the concert. Keep smiling! You have a lovely smile. H.'

Renee was practically shouting down the phone: 'Is there a kiss on it?'

Maggie frowned. She hadn't noticed one at first, but there was something in the swirl of the H's second leg that suggested a possible marking, and yes, if you tilted it a certain way, it resembled a little "x".

'Um, I'm not sure.'

'And you broke your phone so you can't send me a picture. Typical.'

'There's a kind of swirl, but it could be anything.'

'He's shy. He's tried to put one that he could laugh off if you took it the wrong way. Oh, wow. He's smitten. Of course he is. He only had to take one look at you being all weak and needy and he was practically swooning.'

'He was not!'

'Get down to that concert. Now.'

'I just broke up with Dirk. Like, literally hours ago.'

'So? How often does lightening strike? I couldn't give you the official statistics, but I'd guess not too often would just about cover it. Move!'

The line went dead. Maggie actually found herself laughing. She put down the phone and lifted the box, looking through its contents. The little dinner pack had been made with exquisite care. The crusts of the bread had been cut off with careful, deliberate strokes, the cheese neatly spread, the ends of the salad garnish picked off so they didn't protrude too far. It was either the work of someone trying to impress her or with bad OCD. Her mother couldn't have done better.

The phone rang again, startling her. Maggie picked it up, whispering, 'Hello?'

'Get your boots on and get out of there!'

Renee cut the line again. This time, Maggie did as she was told.

25

MUSIC AND COFFEE

THE SNOW WAS GETTING HEAVIER. THE FOOTSTEPS Henry had left were almost buried. Maggie followed them out to the road and saw his trail heading down the centre of the road toward the village square. She was about to follow when a loud bang came from behind her through the trees.

Over the treetops came a flicker of light from the direction of Simon's house. Worried the old man might have started a house fire, Maggie started walking up the street until the street lights became too intermittent, and she was walking in near darkness. Through the trees she could still see a flickering glow.

Something was going on up there, for sure, but she felt an inkling that she wasn't supposed to go that way, that she was supposed to be down at the market with everyone else.

Unable to quell her curiosity, she continued up the

road, trudging through the snow until the first of the buildings came into view.

'Wow.' Maggie's jaw dropped. She gaped, only closing her mouth when the cold air began to make her throat ache.

There, outside Simon's house, sat the most magnificent sleigh she had ever seen. So laden with Christmas lights it was hard to look at directly, it was a beautifully sculpted thing of swirls and curves. It had a large rear platform which was currently empty, and a front seating area large enough for three people to sit side by side.

She was just inching closer to get a better look when a door slammed and footsteps marched out into the snow.

As Simon appeared, dressed in an old trench coat, Maggie ducked back out of sight. The old man walked up to the sleigh, withdrew a cloth from his pocket, and began polishing the wood even as the snow fell over it. Maggie smiled. If it was an elaborate set-up then it was beautifully done, but had someone told her that Simon was actually a pseudonym for Santa Claus she would have found it hard to dispute it.

As though able to read her thoughts, Simon stopped polishing and turned in her direction.

Maggie ducked out of sight. Through a crack in the trees she continued to watch. Simon stared at the light of the trees, then turned and went back into his house.

A moment later the lights on the sleigh blinked off, shrouding the yard in darkness. Maggie turned and made her escape, following the line in the trees that indicated the road until she saw the lights of Hollydell spreading out below her. The snow was falling faster now. She hoped it was heavy enough to hide her tracks should Simon come looking.

She was still thinking about what she had seen when she reached the edge of the village square. It was packed; possibly everyone in Hollydell had assembled here. She spotted Linda and Len across the crowd spread around the stage, and John and Ted standing at the back, eating candy floss. Emma was sitting in the middle, a hotdog in her hands.

A clock over the stage ticked over to six o'clock, and a chime rang out. Everyone cheered as Ellie, dressed in a red Santa jacket, climbed on to the stage and walked to a microphone.

'Welcome, one and all,' she said. 'Christmas is here again, and I'd like to declare the market officially open.'

Another cheer. Around the perimeter, lines of fairy lights blinked on along the roofs of each of the stalls. Some were already open and serving, but those that weren't lifted their outer flaps and switched on their inside lights. Maggie saw everything from burger vans to trinket stalls selling hand-carved Christmas ornaments.

'And now,' Ellie said, 'let the concert begin.'

A group of choir singers dressed in white robes climbed on to the stage. Organ music rang out, and they started into a choral version of *Santa Claus is Coming to Town*, which had the crowd clapping along. Maggie looked around for Henry but couldn't see him. Emma, however, noticed her and gave a frantic wave.

'I saved you a seat, although we'll probably all be dancing later. Are you feeling better?'

Maggie nodded. 'Much,' she said, and genuinely meant it. 'This all looks fantastic.'

'You'll wake up with a stomach-ache from hell, but hey, it's Christmas. And there's a snowman costume relay at nine a.m. tomorrow morning. You might not be able to run too fast, but in those costumes no one can.'

Maggie laughed. 'I'll bear it in mind.'

'Seen Henry yet?'

Maggie frowned. 'I told you, I'm not on the rebound.'

'That's strange, because you've been looking everywhere but at the stage.'

'I was looking at the stalls!' Maggie said, glad the dim lighting hid her blush. 'They look, you know, great.'

'Sure they do. Let's go see what we can find, shall we?'

They headed for the hotdog stands first, because Emma wanted to reload. Halfway there, they bumped into Ted hobbling along on his walking stick on his way to refill two paper cups with hot chocolate. They joined the old man and made a detour, Maggie quietly promising herself to book a dentist appointment for early January.

On the stage, the choir finished their last song and departed to applause. Next up was a group of children acting out a short Christmas nativity. People clapped politely and called out words of encouragement as several children dressed in homemade costumes assembled around the steps up onto the stage.

'Honestly, you could believe they'd ground the cacao beans only this afternoon,' Ted said, taking his first sip of hot chocolate.

'You know that fresh cacao is extremely bitter, don't you?' Emma said. 'And it's not even brown, but kind of off-white.'

Ted laughed. 'Where would the world be without food colouring?'

'We are a society dominated by sugar,' Emma said. 'And it doesn't even grow in the UK.' She winked at Maggie. 'Still, it's Christmas. Oh, and look who's just appeared.'

Henry was standing in the shadows by the side of the stage, watching the nativity. Maggie immediately shrank back beneath the hot chocolate stall's awning.

'Go,' Emma said. 'Go forth and speak.'

'I don't know what to say.'

'Start with "hello" and take it from there. Believe me, the best way to mend a broken heart is with some decent reindeer-farming glue.'

'Don't pressure the poor girl,' Ted said.

'Ah, a bit of pressure never hurt anyone,' John said. 'Ask him for a Christmas kiss. There must be a bit of mistletoe around here somewhere.'

'No!'

Maggie slapped a hand over her mouth, realizing she had shouted the word right at the moment the music had paused, and several people had turned to look at her. She glanced at the side of the stage and saw Henry lift a hand.

'No choice now,' Emma said. 'Go on, girl. Go and meet your destiny.'

'He's not my destiny—'

'Go!'

Hollydell itself seemed to be pushing her toward Henry. Had a reindeer appeared right at that moment, Maggie had no doubt it would have nosed her in the back. Henry, for his part, looked equally awkward as Maggie eased her way through the crowd to where he stood.

'Hi,' he said.

'Hi. Um, I just wanted to say thanks for patching me up yesterday. And for the hamper you left me. It was very thoughtful.'

He smiled and looked away. Was he blushing? On the stage, one little boy dressed as Joseph was handing a doll wrapped in towels to a little girl dressed as Mary. The crowd clapped politely as three children dressed as wise men and three dressed as shepherds began to sing *Away in a Manger* in charmingly high-pitched voices.

'I'm sorry about that,' Henry said. 'Well, actually, I don't mean I'm sorry because I wanted to do it, but I'm sorry I just dropped it and ran. I thought I was going to be late. And I heard you talking on the phone, so I didn't want to disturb you.'

'It's okay.'

'I'm glad you came down. I didn't know if you would.'

'I wouldn't have missed it for the world. I would have borrowed one of the sledges from next door's front garden if I'd had to. When will you play?'

'In about half an hour. There's another choir performance first. Would you like to, um, get some mulled coffee?'

'What's that?'

'It's a Hollydell speciality. It's basically coffee with booze and spices in it.'

'I'm amazed anyone who comes here leaves without having a heart attack.'

'I guess it's all the walking.'

Maggie smiled. 'I heard about the snowman costume relay tomorrow morning. Are you taking part in that?'

Henry laughed. 'No more snowman costumes for me. That was a one-off. In any case, tomorrow is my busiest day. I have to prepare the reindeer for the big Christmas extravaganza.'

'What does that entail? I saw—' Maggie stopped herself before mentioning the sleigh. She felt like a kid revealing to a younger sibling that Santa Claus was indeed an imaginary character.

'You saw…?'

'Um, just a schedule, but I've forgotten what it said.'

'Oh. Well, you'll have to wait and see. Be here by seven, though, otherwise you'll miss out.'

'I'll do my best.'

Henry lifted a hand and held it out to her. Even though they were both wearing gloves, her heart gave a little flutter as she took it. She felt his hand shaking slightly through the combined material. Either he was cold or as nervous as she.

He led her around the side of the square to a little

stall in a corner. He ordered two coffee specials from a rosy-cheeked server and handed one steaming cup to Maggie. The scent of spices was so strong it made her nose itch, but she was still holding Henry's hand with her free hand and didn't want to release it to scratch. Instead, she wrinkled her nose, hoping he wouldn't see.

'It's got quite a pungency, hasn't it?' he said, smiling. 'It'll clear out your sinuses, that's for sure.'

Maggie took a sip. A hint of Irish cream mixed with cinnamon and an under layer of coffee.

'Wow. I'll have another one, please.'

'You haven't drunk that one yet!'

Maggie smiled. 'Oh, but I will. It's lovely.'

'I thought you'd like it. The vendors try to outdo themselves here in Hollydell. Every year we have more amazing Christmas goods than the last.'

Maggie shook her head. 'I still can't believe this place. It's like a wild dream. I mean, I've had my head muddled a little the last few days, but I'm starting to snap out of it now.'

'I noticed that your boyfriend isn't with you.'

Maggie looked down. 'I think we broke up. He found someone else. He didn't want to tell me, but my best friend went down to London and confronted him.'

'Oh. Not much of a Christmas present.'

Maggie shook her head. 'I half expected it, but it still came as a shock. I mean, we haven't seen much of each other in the months since he moved down to London.'

'Oh?'

Maggie took another sip of the coffee. The alcohol

was going to her head, and even though she tried to stop herself talking about Dirk in front of the kind of man most women dreamed about, her tongue was like a runaway train, wagging away with a mind of its own.

'Renee—that's my best friend—never liked him. She always said I could do better, but I thought we were happy, you know. Then he got his big posh job and moved to London. We spoke daily for the first week or so, then his calls and messages stopped. He came back for one weekend in October, but it wasn't quite the same. Something had changed. After that I rarely heard from him. I thought he outgrew me. Perhaps I embarrassed him. He's got some big job, and I'm just a lowly shop assistant—'

Henry's finger pressed against her mouth. At some point during her diatribe he had put down his coffee and removed his glove. His finger was warm, the skin soft.

'No man in his right mind would be embarrassed by you,' he said.

'Um, I ... I....'

Henry stroked her cheek then lowered his hand. Maggie stared at him, her hands shaking, her heart thumping.

'If you ask me, this guy's the one who's lost out,' he said.

Maggie opened her mouth to reply, but something strange was happening. Henry appeared to be shrinking, becoming smaller, the crowd moving in to take him away from her.

'I'll be back in a moment,' he said.

He smiled once then turned away. A curtain beside the stage lifted, and then he was gone. Maggie stared after him, finally understanding as four elderly ladies carrying ornate candlesticks climbed onto the stage. One introduced the others then herself, then they broke into an a cappella rendition of *Have Yourself a Merry Little Christmas* which had the crowd humming with appreciation.

Maggie, replaying her brief conversation with Henry over and over, retreated to the back of the crowd, where she found Emma standing with John and Ted. Linda had wandered over too, while Gail was moving through the crowd nearby with a box of gloves, hats and scarves, handing them out to anyone who looked cold. Overhead, the snow continued to fall steadily like a gentle white shower.

'Well?' Emma demanded.

'Well what?'

'I saw you holding his hand. You're shameless, Maggie Coates. I'm so proud of you.'

'We just had coffee, that's all.'

'What did he say?'

'Oh, not much.'

'Yeah, right.' Emma glared at the stage. 'You can confess after karaoke.'

'Karaoke?'

'You missed it last night. You're not showing us up tonight. Barney's expects.'

Maggie laughed. 'I'm a terrible singer.'

'So? You think John and Ted can really pull off the

Righteous Brothers? My ears were bleeding. Hilarious watching them try.'

'All right, I'll come. Do you think I could bring Henry?'

'Of course. You can do John Travolta and Olivia Newton-John or Elton and Kiki. It'll be a right laugh.'

'We're barely even friends!'

'Ah, but this is Christmas. Now you've got that jerk out of your life, it's time to live it up a little.'

'I don't—'

'Shh! Here he comes.'

The four ladies had left the stage. The crowd went quiet as the curtain opened and Henry stepped out, carrying his acoustic guitar. A stagehand brought out a stool and adjusted his microphone, and Henry sat down.

'Good evening and Merry Christmas,' he said.

'He's so handsome,' John said, getting an elbow in his ribs from Ted. 'If I was forty years younger....'

'Quiet!' Emma hissed.

'Thank you, everyone, for coming to Hollydell this year,' Henry said, his voice measured and easy but containing a hint of nervousness that made Maggie ache to be beside him. 'As you'll all know by now, Hollydell is a special place, but without each and every one of you it wouldn't be anything but an invisible village in a valley in the mountains. You are what makes Hollydell special.'

Cheers came from the audience. Emma did a wolf-whistle so close to Maggie's ear that it made her wince. A couple of people turned around, frowning, and Emma hooked a thumb toward Maggie and shrugged. Maggie wished it would snow even harder.

'I'd like to dedicate this first song to a young lady in the audience,' Henry continued. 'Maggie Coates. She sprained her ankle yesterday but still made it down to be with us for tonight's event. Maggie, this one's for you.'

Maggie cupped her face with her hands. She wasn't sure what was better: having a song dedicated to her or being described as young. Beside her, Emma was making puking motions. Henry, unable to see her through the snow, began a gentle rendition of *Silent Night*, his fingers so smooth across the guitar they were like liquid flowing over glass. The crowd were stunned into silence. Aside from the guitar, the only sound came from the hum of the stall's power generators and the soft patter of the falling snow.

'He gets better every year,' Ted whispered at Maggie's shoulder.

'I wonder how he uses his hands on a woman,' Emma said, leaning close. 'Play your cards right and you might find out.'

Maggie scowled. The truth was, she had begun to consider it. Henry was kind and gentle, and only a bit strange. He said nice things, and he knew when to listen. He was a perfect man.

Emma, John, and Ted were transfixed by the performance. None of them noticed when Maggie stepped quietly backward, slipping between two stalls and away out of the square.

26

WORDS IN THE PARK

MAGGIE WALKED AROUND THE VILLAGE HALL AND headed up the street. The snow was getting heavier, and without anyone clearing the roads it was now halfway up to her knees. She wondered whether she might get snowed in to Comfort Cottage overnight, and how easy it would be to climb out of an upstairs window with a bruised ankle.

With a smile, she figured it was probably best not to think about it.

She walked a little way up the street then turned into the entrance to the park. Everything was covered with snow, but up near the top of the gentle slope a line of benches were partly sheltered by the trees. She wiped the snow off one and sat down, looking down the hill at the brightly lit village.

It was getting easier, but she wasn't ready to jump into anything yet. Dirk's betrayal was still fresh in her mind, and while it would be easy to throw herself into a holiday fling, she feared feeling cheap or getting used. Renee wouldn't care, but Maggie wasn't like her best friend.

Plus, she liked Henry. He was a delightful man, and she didn't want him to get the wrong impression. There were signs that he liked her, but she wasn't about to force herself on him, despite the best efforts of Emma and the others.

Still, the coffee was good. And the smell of his fingers, and the strength in his hand, and the kindness in his eyes—

'Pack it in, Maggie.'

She took a deep breath. She was overreacting, that was all. Henry was just being friendly, helping to cheer her up when she was feeling down. All she had to do was play it casual, keep on her feet and not tumble at his again, and everything would be fine. The concert was in full swing. The market was loaded with delicious food, and everyone was smiling and happy.

There was nowhere better she could be at Christmas except right here.

She sighed. Part of her still missed Dirk. And she usually got together with Renee over Christmas too. It wouldn't be the same this year, no matter what happened.

'Come on, Maggie,' she told herself. 'Snap out of it. Get back down there and enjoy yourself.'

Or she could go the other way. She could shamelessly flirt with Henry, see if he was interested in a holiday romance. Perhaps that was the ticket to making herself feel better.

She stood up, stepped forward, and immediately slipped onto her bum, her legs in the air as she slid down the snowy hillside, coming to rest near the swings at the bottom. She sat up, looking around, hoping no one had seen her utterly humiliating slip-slide. Then, seeing the wide line in the snow and how it had piled over her legs, completely covering her, she did the only reasonable thing that someone could do in such an absurd situation.

She began to laugh.

'Are you all right?'

Maggie turned. Andrew was leaning over the fence, a shovel propped up beside him. His cheeks were red and his forehead shone with sweat.

'Sorry; I fell over.'

'Oh! Did you hurt yourself?'

'No, I'm fine. It was just a slip, that's all.'

Andrew smiled as he came in through the gate. He propped his shovel up against the frame of a seesaw and helped Maggie back to her feet.

'I was just clearing the paths up to the cottages for when the guests head home,' he said. 'I heard someone laughing. I was surprised to see you, to be honest. I know you've not had the best time of late.'

'News gets around, doesn't it?'

Andrew smiled. 'It depends how many people you tell when you're tipsy. But yeah, Hollydell doesn't do secrets very well. Only the important ones.'

Maggie thought about all the advice her new friends had given her over the last few days. A summary would be to stop moping and seize the day. She was still a little disorientated from the fall, so she steeled herself and blurted, 'Why's your brother single? I mean, not that I'm interested or anything—although … well, anyway— but he's such a nice man, and you'd think he'd have a dozen suitors every year.'

Andrew smiled. 'So you finally plucked up the courage to ask the question.'

'What does that mean?'

'I've been here long enough to read people pretty well. I'm not just a train driver, postman, snow-clearer, and about thirty other things.' He laughed. 'I'm a trained psychologist, believe it or not. Even if I wasn't, I could tell from the moment you arrived that you weren't running from something, but you were looking for something new.'

'I was waiting for my boyfriend.'

'What boyfriend doesn't show up to a romantic Christmas getaway? You were broken up bar the public statement.'

'That's not true!'

Andrew planted hands on his hips and cocked his head. With his beard, slightly balding pate and round belly, he looked like a natural father.

'Maggie … come on, be honest. Weren't you a little relieved when Dirk didn't show up? Did you think I didn't notice you down at the station? I know every shadow, every cubbyhole of that place. You might have thought that you were waiting for him, but you weren't. You were trying to see if there was a break.'

Maggie felt uncomfortable under his gaze. 'I don't believe you, but what if I was?'

'You came to Hollydell to move forward with your

life, not to try to repair your past. You're not the first, and you won't be the last. And now you have that chance.' He smiled. 'The world is yours. You can take what you want.'

'You haven't answered my question….'

Andrew laughed again. 'About Henry? Oh, he's single. He's been single since his wife left him.'

'His wife? He was married?'

'Yeah, seven years. No kids. They both had careers. Hers took her overseas, and without her, his lost its meaning. He came back to Hollydell to recover his senses. And once back here, he decided he liked the quiet life. It doesn't matter how many numbers you have in a bank account, you see. It's how full your soul is.'

'His wife left him because of her career?'

Andrew shook his head. 'Oh man, she was a witch. She sucked him dry, twisted him into a person I barely recognised. When she finally spat him out, she told him he was too boring and sent him on his way. He later found out she'd been having affairs with several other men she met online. She didn't even both to hide it, but that's one reason he's happy here where we live in an internet black spot. He doesn't have to worry about any of that social media rubbish.'

Maggie shook her head. 'She sounds horrible. Poor Henry. How could she possibly have thought he was boring? He's probably the most interesting man I've ever met.'

Andrew shrugged. 'Well, you know what they say? One man's trash is another's treasure, and all that.'

'When was this?'

'Oh, a few years ago. He was in his late twenties. He came back to live in Hollydell, and settled here, taking over Father's reindeer farm and generally pottering around. He suits himself. Sometimes he travels during the summer, or attends courses in Inverness or down in Edinburgh, but he determined never to have his heart broken again.'

'So he doesn't do holiday romances?'

'Not at all. It's the last thing he's interested in. He's a qualified vet with a specialisation in equestrian animals. He writes poetry and classical guitar music. He has a tournament chess rating of nearly two thousand, which might mean nothing to you, but in the chess world it's semi-professional.' Andrew laughed. 'Seriously, my brother is a king among nerds. He barely knows how to talk to women. Grotbags was his first proper girlfriend.'

'Grotbags?'

Andrew shrugged. 'That was my name for her. I think it was Geraldine.'

Maggie was silent for a moment. 'Poor Henry,' she said again.

Andrew looked at his watch. 'I'd better get back to work. There's a fireworks display in about twenty minutes, after which everyone will head off to other events or go home. They'll all be a bit tipsy, and that's when most slips happen. Be careful tomorrow. The snow's likely to get a lot worse. We've had a lot this year, even for here.'

'Thank you for your kind words, Andrew.'

Andrew smiled. 'You know what? There's something I need to tell you. I don't go much on meddling in people's affairs, but deep down my brother is pretty lonely. He'd love someone in his life. As in a real person, not a reindeer or a cat. He has plenty of those already. I know he doesn't go in for holiday flings, but you're all he's talked about since you showed up.'

'Me?'

'When I'm with him he talks about you constantly. I had to tell him to shut up when we were fixing one of the runners on Father's sleigh because he was doing my head in. You know he's been calling me every day to see if your boyfriend's come in on the train?'

'I didn't know that.'

'He's smitten, Maggie. Honestly, I can see why. Toss out the negativity and you're a wonderful person.'

'Um, thanks.'

'It's a shame you won't be sticking around after Christmas. You're leaving on the twenty-seventh?'

'I promised my friend I'd meet up with her. We have a regular Christmas Eve date together, but this year I'll be missing it. We moved it to the day after Boxing Day.'

'It's a shame you can't get her to come up here to Hollydell.'

'She works for a children's charity. She can't leave her kids.'

Andrew nodded. 'Well, if you have a chance, please talk to my brother. He's not one for the internet, but he likes writing letters.'

'Letters?' Maggie laughed. 'As in with actual paper?'

'He was a total embarrassment at school. I was in the wrestling club. He sat alone in the library every lunchtime studying copperplate handwriting. Picture the biggest nerd you could ever imagine, and double it, and you've got my brother.'

Maggie couldn't keep the smile off her face. 'Can he knit?'

'Several different stitches. When he was a poor student he used to knit sweaters for our Christmas presents. He can crochet and darn too.'

'Oh my.'

'Next time you see him, ask him about his jam. He makes his own.'

Maggie giggled. 'He sounds like my grandmother.'

'I'm not trying to put you off, by the way. My brother is a wonderful person. But you know, be aware what you're getting into. Sorry, I really need to go.'

Maggie nodded. 'Thank you, Andrew,' she said.

He patted her on the shoulder. 'Good luck.'

27

RESOLUTIONS

'WHERE DID YOU GET TO?' EMMA SAID. 'YOUR mulled wine's gone cold. Come on, you're playing catch-up.'

Maggie took the paper cup and sipped the spicy liquid. 'I went for a walk.'

'I thought you might have been snogging Henry behind the bike sheds.'

'Henry? No. Where is he?'

'He packed up his guitar case and headed up the street. I thought you must have arranged something.'

Maggie shook her head. 'No, nothing.'

Emma shrugged. 'Must have been tired. Never mind. We have karaoke after this. Mates before dates.'

'Um, sure.'

'Scull it.'

'What?'

'The wine. We'll get one more in, then watch the

fireworks and head up to Barney's. You're not considering chickening out, are you? Miss New-Leaf?'

Emma was quite clearly sloshed, swaying from side to side, blinking with great emphasis, her cheeks glowing.

Maggie smiled. 'I wouldn't miss it for the world.' It did sound like fun, even though Henry's abrupt departure was playing on her mind. Perhaps he had looked for her and thought she had already gone home.

The last performer had left the stage. Ellie appeared, a microphone in one hand, a paper cup of a hot, steaming liquid in the other.

'Thank you, everyone, for coming tonight,' she said. 'It's been a wonderful night. Take care going home or on to your next port of call, and we'll see you in the morning. It's Christmas Eve in ten … nine … eight ….'

The crowd started counting down. Maggie couldn't believe midnight had come so quickly.

'… two … one … Merry Christmas!'

A line of fireworks rose up into the sky from behind the stage. Most of the colour was lost in the snow, but the bangs rang out over the cheers of the crowd.

'Right, let's go,' Emma said, taking Maggie's arm. 'We need a seat near the TV so I can read the words.'

John and Ted turned out to do a pretty good Righteous Brothers impression. Emma, after one incredible turn as Tina Turner doing *What's Love Got To Do With It?*, passed out on a sofa chair and snored so loudly Linda turned up the music's volume. Gail, off duty, knew all the words to every Lady Gaga song in the karaoke book, even if her voice was more of a parrot-like screech, while Jim the town crier was nearly note perfect on a succession of stage musical standards.

Maggie, for her part, battled her way through a Donna Summer track before slaughtering some Bee Gees, then retired to a corner chair to enjoy the show and get quietly drunk.

It was after two when she finally stumbled through the door of Comfort Cottage and pulled off her boots. The snow was twenty centimetres deep on the road outside and still coming down, even though she had followed a depression which showed where Andrew had gone with the plough sometime earlier.

The cottage was freezing, so she threw a couple of logs onto the embers of the fire and sat on the nearest armchair with her legs bunched up under a thick tartan blanket.

There had been a message on the answerphone from Renee, wishing her Merry Christmas, and as Maggie sat watching the flames crackle in the grate she realised she was feeling much better about everything.

Dirk could go to hell. She only wished Henry had stuck around, although in light of her karaoke performances, it was perhaps good that he hadn't.

Hollydell was wonderful, her new friends were lovely, and there was a dishy geek who seemed to like her.

Everything was perfect except for one small thing: she only had two days left.

Renee would tell her to seize the day, and Andrew

had told her how much Henry liked her. If anything was going to happen between them, she didn't have much time left to act.

The fire was crackling in the grate now, the room filling with warmth. She understood how Comfort Cottage got its name, and she pulled her legs up under her, nestling her face against the armchair's back.

There really was magic here in Hollydell. It was subtle, hiding away until you needed it, but it was definitely there. She could feel it weaving around her, calming and soothing her. Or was that just the residue of the wine?

She got up and checked the fire guard was set properly, and then crawled back under her blanket. Perhaps she would just sleep here tonight, with the fire's warmth bathing her, dreaming of the perfect man who lived up the road, his strong arms around her, his body pressed against her….

28

RESCUE

THE ROOM WAS COLD WHEN SHE WOKE. A FEW EMBERS still flickered in the fire, so Maggie climbed stiffly out from under her blanket and got it started again. Daylight peeped through a crack in the curtains, and when she pulled them open she was dazed by a field of glowing white.

The snow was still dumping down, the drifts on the fence posts thirty centimetres or more.

The clock said a little after eight. The snowman relay started at nine, so she didn't have much time if she was going to participate.

Her head felt a little muggy, and she'd had only about five hours' sleep, but the moment she opened the front door the crisp chill of the morning invigorated her.

The little hamper Henry had made her still sat on the telephone table. She didn't have time to get breakfast at Barney's or one of the other restaurants, so she took the hamper back into the kitchen, sat down on one of the stools, and slowly ate while waiting for the kettle to boil.

She could quite believe what Andrew had claimed after taking a few bites. The food was exquisite, prepared with exactly the right amount of salt and spices to bring out every flavour. Everything had been prepared down to a fine detail; even the angles of the bread could have been cut with a set square.

In a few minutes the box was empty. Maggie stared at it, realising she had her excuse to visit Henry. The snowman relay could wait; she really needed to return the hamper.

She drank a strong cup of coffee then packed the wooden hamper into a plastic bag so it wouldn't get wet. The bruise on her ankle still ached, but the colour had faded a little from yesterday, and it didn't hurt so much to slide it into the boot. She might yet be dancing later today; with Henry if things worked out right.

The snow was deep and still falling as she headed out, wading up the street. Downhill, the lights of Hollydell were almost obscured by the blizzard, and when she reached Simon's place around the curve she found all the buildings shut up. The tunnel cutting through the hillside offered a brief respite from the storm despite its gloom, but when she emerged by Henry's reindeer farm all she saw was another blanket of white.

Henry's house appeared out of the snow like a mirage. Maggie immediately frowned, sensing something was wrong. *Trust your instincts,* Renee would say, and Maggie's instinct told her something bad had happened.

The front door was open, a line of footprints heading around the house's rear toward the field. As Maggie approached she saw what had unnerved her: they were already starting to fill in, but they went one way only.

There were no footprints coming back.

Whatever had made him leave the house in such a hurry to not shut his front door in the face of a vicious snowstorm had also kept him from returning.

Miffy was sitting on the mat, looking out at the snow. Maggie gave the cat a pat on the head, and it mewed in greeting. A quick glance inside told her that Henry's boots were gone, but his coat still hung on a rack inside the door.

Wherever he had gone, he hadn't expected to be gone long.

His footsteps were starting to fill up with snow.

Maggie turned and headed back out, following the footsteps, careful not to disturb them in case she lost the trail. They headed around the back, across a small farmyard and though a gate.

Several reindeer watched her from inside a shed, but an oil drum had been rolled up against the gate to hold it shut.

The gate must have broken. One of them must have got out.

The footprints led to the main field at the farm's

rear. It undulated between two lines of trees then dropped out of sight down a hillside into a valley.

The line of footprints led straight across.

'Henry!' Maggie shouted, jogging through the snow. 'Henry, are you there?'

Out in the middle of the field, with the blizzard raging, Maggie was surrounded on all sides by white. She felt a sudden acute sense of panic, but the trail of Henry's footprints—although almost filled in—still led straight ahead. She broke into the best run she could in nearly knee-deep snow, ignoring the throb of her ankle, wanting only to find something, anything that wasn't snow or white.

The hillside steepened, and a couple of times she stumbled, sliding through the snow. Henry's trail was easier to follow here, as she could see he had done the same, the snow pushed into thick drifts where he had half-slid, half-rolled.

And then spindly shadows appeared out of the blizzard, the skeletal outlines of trees bent like old men under their weight of snow.

The field was so steep down to the line of trees that Maggie had to slide. She saw a fence backing on to the nearest trees, but there, farther along the tree line it had bucked under a broken bough that had fallen across it.

Henry's footprints led that way.

'Henry!' she screamed, climbing over the collapsed fence and pushing through the brush beneath the trees. Here, the snow wasn't as deep, but she had the undergrowth to deal with and the exposed roots of trees hidden under the snow.

The hillside steepened even more, until Maggie was using the boughs of the trees to support herself as she climbed down. Henry's trail was still easy to follow, his tracks a jagged line through otherwise pristine snow.

The hillside was dipping into a valley. From ahead came the roar of rushing water.

'Henry!' she screamed.

Then, over the water, she heard Henry shout back: 'Maggie! Down here!'

The roar of the water was deafening by the time she finally saw him among trees that overhung a mountain stream gushing through rocks laden with snow. He wore only a sweater, and he was braced between two saplings, his arms straining on a rope that stretched taut down to the river.

'Take the end! Tie it! I can't hold her much longer!'

Maggie scrambled down a few more steps and finally saw what was on the other end of the rope. George, her fur soaked, was stuck in a gully, her legs dangling out over the river. A muddy trail of disturbed snow showed where the reindeer had slid down the steep riverbank.

Henry had secured a harness around her body, but the reindeer had slipped farther, and now hung just a couple of metres above the raging waters.

'There,' Henry shouted. 'Take that bit of slack. Tie it to that sapling over there. Quickly, as tight as you can.'

Maggie grabbed the rope. It was crusted with ice and mud. She scrambled across the riverbank to the tree Henry had indicated and looped the rope around it, tying it in a tight knot.

'Got it.'

'And the other, if you can reach.'

She took the slack of the other rope and did the same. Henry tested their weight before releasing them, then began climbing down the riverbank to where George was stuck. Maggie shifted forward until she could see Henry at the reindeer's side, carefully working his hands around George's body, easing the deer free.

'When I call, pick up the slack on those ropes, Maggie,' Henry said. 'Brace yourself on something. She might have an injury. I can't tell yet.'

George snorted and whinnied as Henry soothed her, his hands working to get her free. Then, with a sudden jolt, George found purchase with her front legs. Henry pushed her from behind and she was free.

'Now, Maggie!'

Maggie pulled on the ropes, wrapping them around her arm. Part pulled, part pushed, and part on her own efforts, George scrambled up the slope until she reached the trees. The reindeer whinnied at Maggie, who grabbed the top of her harness until a muddy Henry reached them.

'Give me a moment. I need to examine her. Hold the harness for me.'

Maggie nodded. Henry, frowning, ran his hands over George's body. The reindeer was remarkably compliant as Henry felt everywhere from her neck and ribs down to her hooves. At last he looked up at Maggie and his face cracked into a smile.

'A couple of scratches, that's all. She'll be fine. Nice

to see you, Maggie. You picked a perfect moment to stop by.'

His eyes were full of relief. Maggie found hers glazing with tears as she said, 'I just came to bring your hamper box back.'

29

DISAPPOINTMENTS

THE SNOW WAS EASING A LITTLE AS THEY WALKED back across the field, Maggie's footprints providing a trail to follow. Henry held George's bridle, while Maggie carried the harness. All three of them were covered from head to foot in mud and snow. Henry and Maggie had suffered a few cuts and bruises, but George looked remarkably well as she trotted along between them.

'She's a feisty one,' Henry laughed. 'I heard the gate go, and knew it would be her. The bolt was a bit loose, but she must have given it a real hit. I couldn't have anticipated that tree going down over the fence.'

'What was she doing down there?'

'Looking for food. You showed up at the perfect time. I managed to get that harness around her, but she slipped out of my hands and nearly went in. That river is treacherous.' He shook his head. 'I should have checked the fence better. I went round the pastures only a week ago.'

'You can't allow for a storm like this.'

Henry shrugged. 'I should have checked.'

Maggie smiled. 'No harm done, is there? What is it Shakespeare would say? All's well that ends well.'

Henry smiled. 'I didn't know you were a fan.'

'I've seen the movie.'

Henry laughed as George nudged Maggie in the ribs. 'I think she likes you.'

'Of course she does. What's not to like?'

Henry smiled and looked away. When he looked back, he said, 'How about we get cleaned up and then I treat you to breakfast? And since you're so good with the reindeer, perhaps you can help me get them ready.'

'What for?'

Henry smiled. 'To pull Father's sleigh. George is making her debut this year.'

'Simon?'

'You haven't seen Christmas until you've seen Christmas Eve in Hollydell,' Henry said. 'But you can't see it dressed like that. Neither can I, for that matter.'

Henry's farmhouse appeared out of the snowstorm, a boxy shadow easing into detail.

'I've got to clean George and give her a proper check,' Henry said. 'Just to make sure she's all right. I'll be half an hour or so. Why don't you go into the house and get cleaned up? There are towels in the bathroom cupboard.'

'My clothes are a mess.'

Henry laughed. 'I noticed. I'm not sure if I'll have anything your size, but you can take anything you find from my closet that you like. I'm afraid it's mostly overalls, and the odd snowman costume.'

Maggie grinned. 'I might make the relay if I'm quick about it.'

Henry smiled then led George off toward the shed. Maggie was freezing and dirty on the outside, but on the inside she felt only a warm, comforting glow.

Around the front, she found all of Henry's cats waiting on the front step. They greeted her like an old friend, before doing their catlike business and demanding food. Maggie stripped off her jacket and wiped her trousers down as best she could, then headed for the kitchen. She hoped Henry wouldn't mind if she sorted their food before dealing with herself.

None of the open shelves held any cat food so she had no choice but to look into some of his cupboards. She found a neat array of food, some of the posher supermarket brands plus some less common local goods. She wanted to nose around even more, but the cats wouldn't let up, so eventually she found a box of dry food in a cupboard above the sink. As she removed it, she noticed a jar of Waitrose strawberry jam. It was only half full, and there were no other jars.

Strange, she thought, considering Andrew had said his brother made his own.

A couple of the cats were making walking extremely difficult. Maggie filled their bowls then replaced the box and headed for the bathroom.

Half an hour later, she was sitting in the living room wearing a loosely fitting pair of Henry's jeans and a sweater that was at least two sizes too big. It hung down over her hips and the arms flopped loose around hers.

The door opened and Henry came in. He had already cleaned up a bit, and was wearing white overalls.

'Hey,' he said, smiling. 'Thanks again. You have no idea how lucky it was that you showed up. Both me and George could have ended up in that river.'

Maggie shrugged. 'It was nothing.'

'And my clothes really suit you,' he said. 'I can lend you some more if you like.'

'No! Although they're pretty warm.'

'I'm afraid it's always cold in Hollydell. Even in summer. I'll just get changed. Help yourself to coffee or tea. Anything you can find.'

'Thanks.'

Maggie got up and went through to the kitchen. The sound of the shower drifted through the wall as she boiled the kettle and made herself some coffee. She had forgotten to ask Henry how he liked it, so she left him a cup on the side and headed back to the living room.

At the doorway she paused. The adjacent door to the study was ajar.

Maggie bit her lip. The shower was still going, so he would never know if she had a little look around. Henry was like a horde of buried treasure being teased up one coin at a time, and Maggie couldn't resist the urge to cup her hands into the dirt.

She set the coffee down on a hall table and went inside. A notebook was open in front of a computer on a desk. Maggie crept closer, making out lines of text. Was this the poetry Andrew had talked about?

From the bathroom, the shower noise cut off. Panicking, Maggie darted forward, narrowly avoiding catching her foot on an extension cord that stretched across the floor. She had time for one quick glance at the text on the open page before retreating to the hall.

She frowned, disappointed. Not the Wordsworth or TS Eliot she'd hoped for, but a list of dry feed ledgers, delivery dates, and suppliers' fees.

Typical farmer's accounting work.

She got herself back to the kitchen just as the bathroom door opened. Maggie turned, letting out a little gasp to find Henry naked to the waist and still wet, wearing only a towel. Gasping almost as loud, he ducked out of sight back into the bathroom.

'Sorry!' he said though the door. 'I thought you were in the living room.'

'Um, I was … um, sugar?'

Henry laughed. 'Just milk. I'll be out in a moment.'

'I'll wait in the living room. I promise!'

'Thanks!'

Maggie felt a little hot around the neck as she took their coffees back to the living room and set them down on a table. She had got only a glimpse of Henry, but she had caught sight of a chest and shoulders chiselled through hard labour. She'd never cared much about a man's body, but it certainly added another dimension. So what if he didn't make his own jam or write poetry?

Or perhaps those powerful arms and broad shoulders did matter. Perhaps they mattered a lot.

But if he didn't really write poetry or made his own jam, what else might Andrew have lied about?

Andrew claimed Henry had talked about her all the time.

What if he'd been lying about that too, in some crude attempt to match-make for his single brother? Henry might not like her at all. Renee had always claimed three cats was the maximum allowed for a sane person. After that, things begin to go downhill.

The door opened and Henry came in, dressed in jeans and a sweater. 'Sorry about that,' he said. 'I'm not used to a woman being in the house. Sometimes my mother stops by and lets herself in, but you know, she's seen it all.'

'I didn't see quite everything,' Maggie said, then slapped a hand over her mouth. 'I mean—'

'Don't worry,' Henry said. 'It's fine. Ah, you made coffee. Thank you. I feel pretty bad about you doing so much for me after helping with George. You could have been hurt. Hollydell is a beautiful place, but those gully streams are treacherous.'

'You could have been hurt too.'

Henry nodded. 'Thanks to you I wasn't. I lost a couple of deer to that stream before we got the fence up. Comes with the territory, I'm afraid.' He clapped his hands together. 'Are you ready for breakfast? My treat. I know a quiet little café on the outskirts of the village.'

'It sounds nice.'

Henry grinned. 'Only as nice as the company. So, I guess, it is.'

30

CAFÉ

HENRY SUGGESTED THEY WALK BECAUSE IN THE SNOW it was hard to do anything else. With Henry insisting on holding her hand in case she slipped, they made their way along the forest road back to the village, where in places the snow had drifted nearly waist deep. Henry offered to carry Maggie if her ankle started to hurt, and while having seen his muscles she didn't doubt he was capable, she still wasn't sure how he felt about her. The one or two times he had said anything that sounded like a line, it had come across as awkward and forced, as though he had read them in a book but never used them in real life. And for her part, the confidence blow Dirk's betrayal had given her meant she couldn't take anything for certain ever again.

The café was as delightful as Henry had promised, a log cabin set back from the road with a Christmas tree sitting on an outer deck and tinsel glittering in the windows. A high ceiling inside was decorated with fairy lights and antique Christmas ornaments nestled on the crossbeams. The owner, a man with a German accent who wore a name-tag announcing him as Fredrick, greeted Henry like an old friend and led them to a nice table close to an open fire. An old Labrador retriever sleeping on a fluffy rug lifted one eyelid as they sat down, then went back to sleep.

'How's old Arthur doing?' Henry asked Fredrick as he came to take their order.

'Oh, he's two winters past how long I thought he'd go, so I think he's good for a couple more. Dreaming of the summer and rabbits in the fields, no doubt.'

Henry reached down and gave the dog a pat on the head. Arthur whined softly but didn't open his eyes.

'This is Maggie,' Henry said. 'A very dear friend of mine.'

Maggie balked at the use of "friend" but felt an excited tingle at the use of "dear". Henry could hardly call her his girlfriend, could he? She nodded to the dog, muttering, 'Nice to meet you,' before realising Henry was talking to Fredrick.

'Oh, um, hi,' she said, wanting the ground to swallow her up. 'It's very nice to meet you too.'

'We had a little trouble in the fields this morning,' Henry said. 'One of the deer got out. Maggie saved the day. I'd have been in the river had it not been for her.'

Fredrick tipped his chef's hat. 'Delighted to have you visit my little café. Everything's on the house. I'll make you a breakfast special.'

'Thanks so much.'

'And two coffees,' Henry said, running a hand through his hair. 'I'm exhausted.'

As Fredrick headed off to the kitchen, an awkward silence fell over them. Henry looked at Maggie, who looked at him, looked away again, then looked back, only to see him look away.

'It's been a long day,' Henry said.

'Yes,' Maggie said. 'It's only ten o'clock.'

'Yes, it is,' Henry said.

'I like *Clocks*,' Maggie said.

'Oh, that's nice.'

'Um, I mean the song by Coldplay.'

'It's a nice song.'

'Can you play it?'

Henry shrugged. 'I'm not sure. I've never tried.'

Under the table, Maggie tried to kick her feet together, something Renee always did when she was babbling. Instead she managed only to kick Henry.

'Oh, sorry.'

'That's okay.'

'I wasn't—'

'I know.'

Was this what it felt like to be fifteen again? Maggie could still remember her first date, with a guy called Paul Brooks from the upper sixth. She'd been so nervous she'd chugged a can of Diamond White before meeting him in a café, only to then throw up over his dinner. He'd laughed it off, but a second date had never materialised.

'I like the décor,' she said.

'Yes, Fredrick's done it nice. He's hidden twelve toy rcindeer around the room. Can you spot them all?'

Relieved to have something to do to break the awkwardness, Maggie twisted in her chair, counting the stuffed reindeer hiding among other ornaments, between books on shelves, on top of the mantel over the fire.

'I can only find eleven,' Maggie said.

Henry frowned. 'Keep looking. There's another around here somewhere.'

Maggie craned her neck to look around, feeling an absurd fear that her failure to spot all twelve reindeer would be a losing deal in Henry's eyes. Counting only the same eleven as before, she was beginning to panic when she spotted a stack of board games on a shelf in a corner and found an opportunity to change the subject. It might calm her nerves and relieve the tension to play something. She was about to suggest it when she noticed a chess set at the top.

'Um, I heard you play chess,' she said, nodding toward the games.

Henry lifted an eyebrow. 'Is that right?'

'Yeah. I heard you were quite good.'

Henry laughed. 'I was school champion three years in a row.'

Maggie let out a relieved breath. So, at least Andrew hadn't been lying about that. 'That's pretty impressive,' she said.

'Well, you might have noticed there aren't many people around here. I went to a school a couple of villages over. We had to trudge along that trail by the lake, four miles each way, even in the snow. It wasn't a big school; a couple of hundred kids. There were only nine of us in the chess club. I was the only one who knew the names of all the pieces.'

Maggie's hopes sank. 'Oh. And I guess you don't make jam, either.'

Henry leaned forward, a conspiratorial grin on his face. 'You've been talking to my brother, haven't you?'

Maggie started to shake her head, but she could tell from his eyes that he could see the lie before she'd told it. She sighed. 'Yes,' she said. 'He told me lots of things about you that don't seem to be true.'

'He always was the joker in the family,' Henry said.

'I can see that now,' Maggie answered, wanting to sink through the floor.

Fredrick brought the food. On two wide wooden platters, loaded with German sausages, cheeses, and hard breads with several pots of different sauces, the food was delicious. Maggie found herself stuffing it down, getting paranoid about eating too fast, trying not to eat, figuring what the hell, Henry probably didn't even like her, and going for it again anyway. The whole time, Henry watched her over his food with a twinkle of amusement in his eyes.

The food was gone before Maggie knew it. Henry, who had seemed to be eating in a perfectly cultured, methodical manner while she munched like a pig at a trough, had somehow finished just before her. She smiled as she lifted her coffee then slapped a hand over her mouth to hide a burp.

Henry didn't seem to notice, his eyes gazing calmly into hers.

'That was lovely,' she said. 'You don't get food like that down in Cambridge. Well, there's a German restaurant, but I've never been in it. Renee—my best friend—said never to trust a restaurant with cobwebs over the door.'

'A wise decision,' Henry said. 'I'll tell Fredrick to make sure he keeps the entrance clean.'

'No, I didn't mean—'

'I was joking.'

'Oh.'

Henry called Fredrick over. He thanked the chef, who then took away their plates. As Fredrick left, Henry turned to Maggie and said, 'Do you think you could make it from here back to your cottage or into the village? I have a few things to do over at Father's place before this evening.' He smiled. 'Top secret things.'

Maggie's heart sank. So, he didn't like her after all, she was a pig, and he wanted to get rid of her. The previous invitation to help with the reindeer had been withdrawn, and life utterly sucked.

'Sure,' she said, her voice so hollow she could have driven a London bus between her vocal cords. 'If that's what you want.'

'I'll come and find you later,' he said. 'I haven't forgotten my promise.'

Maggie's heart jumped again. 'No? I mean—'

Henry patted her hand. 'We just have to get the boring stuff out of the way. Waxing the sleigh runners, checking the bolts on the rails and the fittings on the harnesses, things like that. It's cold, dirty work, and I think you've seen me dirty enough today already.'

'Um, no—I mean yes—'

Henry laughed. It was such a warm, comforting sound, Maggie could have listened to it all day.

'If you're not busy, sure.'

'I won't forget.'

Fredrick came over to wish them a good day. 'Did you find all eleven reindeer?' he asked.

Maggie turned to Henry. 'You said there were twelve.'

'I thought there were.'

Fredrick shrugged. 'Customer's dog took a shine to one. I didn't have the heart to ask for it back.'

After saying goodbye to Fredrick, they headed out of the restaurant. Henry helped Maggie with her boots and jacket. He went to open the door for her, but paused.

'I just wanted to say thank you again for helping me out this morning,' Henry said. 'You saved me, really.'

Maggie nodded. A few more awkward seconds passed, then Henry smiled.

'And my brother, Andrew, well, he talks too much, but he's not always full of it.' He shrugged. 'I was also university chess champion. There were a lot more players in the club at St. Andrews. I didn't play against Prince William, though. He was probably in the polo team or something.'

'And do you really make your own jam?' Maggie said in a small, mouse like voice.

Henry looked about to burst into laughter, but held

it behind a smile. 'I'll tell you later. Perhaps we could have breakfast together again tomorrow?'

Maggie's heart was beating so hard she couldn't even reply. She stole glances at him as they made their way to the end of the path, where they paused again. Maggie looked up at him, expectant, wondering what would happen. Henry looked into her eyes.

'I, um, don't do holiday romances,' he said.

Maggie felt him take her hand and squeeze it through their gloves.

Make a move on him! screamed Renee's voice in her head. *Come on, this isn't 1950 and he isn't Frank Sinatra! Go for it!*

'How about just this once?' she whispered, her heart thundering so loud she wasn't sure if he had heard her or not. 'I, um, wouldn't mind.'

Henry shook his head. 'No.' Then, with a regretful smile, he added, 'It's the holiday part I don't like.'

He squeezed her hand again then was gone before she could reply, striding off into the snow. Maggie watched him, her lips trembling, wondering what had happened, whether that had been a come-on or a fob-off. The snow was still falling heavily, and while she thought she saw him turn, he was too far away to be more than a shadow.

Then he was gone, and her heart was battering against her ribs so hard she thought it would break out of her chest and chase after him.

She forced herself to turn back toward the village, breathing in the chill winter air to calm herself.

Henry.

He was more than just a man, he was perfection in human form. She couldn't let him escape, not when she had sensed the spark leaping between them. She had to catch up with him, grab him, pull him to her, kiss him, roll over with him in the snow while robins chirped and Christmas lights twinkled until somewhere she heard Bing Crosby singing.

'Excuse me! You over there. Where are we, exactly?'

Maggie turned. A figure in a snowman costume was stumbling out of the blizzard toward her. She laughed as she recognised John's voice.

'Hey, John. The relay still going, is it? I'm afraid I didn't quite make it.'

'Maggie, is that you? Where in Hollydell are we? And what on earth are you wearing?'

'Oh, um….' She bent double, one hand over her mouth, remembering only at that point that she was still wearing Henry's clothes.

'I'm not saying it isn't fetching, rather just a little more masculine than I'd expect.'

'It's a long story,' Maggie said. 'By the way, do you know where Emma is? I need hot chocolate, I need marshmallows, and I have a couple of things I need to tell her about.'

John's chuckle was muffled by the suit. 'I'll do my best to escort you,' he said. 'Don't walk too fast, mind. I've fallen over half a dozen times already.'

31

THE LAST (HEALTHY) SUPPER

MAGGIE FOUND EMMA WITH TED, LINDA, AND LEN IN a snow-covered village square, drinking what was probably not her first glass of mulled wine, and lamenting over how Linda had pulled a number on her up the home straight, bundling her off into the verge to claim victory in a photo finish. John, it seemed, had got lost halfway round and taken a detour that had left him on the other side of the village.

'Well, look who it is,' Emma said. 'Pour the girl a drink. She needs one if that's all she could find to wear. The sweater-and-jeans look. I like it. Very Christmas-casual. Will definitely keep the men away, and they're like vultures at this time of year, preying on the weak and the recently broken-hearted.'

'I got a bit dirty over at Henry's place,' Maggie said.

'What?'

'Not that kind of dirty! Snow and mud and stuff.'

As the others crowded round, Maggie found herself giving a recount of events. Nervous now she was in company, she glossed over their visit to the café for breakfast as best she could, but Emma wouldn't be put off.

'Did he put the hard word on you?'

'No!'

'Oh, he did. I can see it in your eyes.'

'We're just friends.'

'I've heard that before. Just be careful. You're vulnerable at this time of year, especially in your current situation.'

'What situation?' Linda asked, having apparently missed the gossip being passed around.

'Maggie's boyfriend went off with someone else,' Emma said, waving a hand. 'Typical man. No offense, guys.'

John, Ted, and Len gave various shrugs.

'So, it's Christmas Eve,' Maggie said, trying to change the subject. 'What's next on the schedule?'

'Well, thanks to this snow, Ellie's asked if we can all chip in to help clear the square out before tonight's Christmas extravaganza. She and Gail are getting out the shovels as we speak. With your ankle you could probably sit it out if you like, but it's the last chance to get some exercise before the grand Christmas pudding unveiling ceremony.'

'The what?'

'She's a newbie, remember?' John said, rubbing his hands together. 'Oh, I love it when we get a newbie.'

'The Christmas pudding unveiling is a Hollydell

tradition,' Ted said. 'Every year, they make a giant Christmas pudding.'

'How giant?'

'Last year's topped eighty kilograms.'

Maggie was taken aback. 'Are you serious?'

'Everyone in the village gets some. They also have a barrel of clotted cream that's come up from Cornwall. Someone makes a speech or whatever, but no one really pays attention. It's all about the eating. We have to finish the thing because the year's Christmas message is written on the plate.'

'Seriously?' Maggie couldn't keep the grin off her face. 'Sounds amazing.'

Emma shook her head. 'You'd think, wouldn't you? There's always way too much, but Ellie won't let us stop until it's all gone. It's practically torture by the time you're on your third plate.'

'Three?' Linda said. 'I remember you finished five last year.'

Emma gave a solemn nod as she patted her stomach. 'No one can ever say I'm not a team player. I remember you dropped out at four. You let everyone down.'

'They were big plates!'

Emma glanced at Maggie. 'So she says. So she says.'

'I can't wait,' Maggie said. Then, remembering breakfast, she added, 'Well, I could wait a couple of hours, I guess.'

'She's struggling,' John said.

'Maggie, dear, you have to eat through it,' Linda said, in the tone an old grandmother might use when instructing someone how to burn off a corn. 'You can't let your stomach tell you what to do. Not until New Year.'

'I'll do my best.'

In front of them, Ellie had appeared on the stage. There was no microphone, so she clapped her hands together until people turned toward her.

'Hey, everyone, thanks for offering to help. If you could take a spade off Gail over there and just see if we can get this place cleared out a little bit. The forecast looks like the snow will ease toward mid afternoon so we should be good by then.' As they headed off to where Gail was handing out brightly coloured plastic shovels, Ellie clapped her hands again. 'Oh, and by the way, we will be singing Christmas songs while we work. No objections. Does someone want to nominate the first song?'

'The *Hokey Cokey*!' Emma shouted.

Ellie looked surprised. 'Well, I guess we can try. Just be careful when lifting those legs....'

For the next hour, they cleared snow to the garrulous but not altogether tuneful sound of a mix-n-match of Christmas classics and other cheesy chart hits, some of which no one—even the suggester—seemed to know the words of. By the time Ellie called a halt, Maggie's throat was aching.

'We've prepared lunch for everyone,' Ellie shouted from the stage while Gail was collecting the shovels. The snow had eased, and a hint of blue sky shone through the clouds, although heaps of snow now filled every available space. 'If you could all walk around to the main entrance of the village hall, that would be great.'

Inside, Maggie found Phillip from the delicatessen and Sally from the dog sled tours presiding over a long trestle table heaped with a remarkably healthy lunch buffet. A few raisins in the salad offered the only sugar on offer among plates of lightly cured meats, slices of cheese, heaps of olives, salads, and boiled potatoes in a basil garnish. Maggie turned to Emma, one eyebrow raised.

'Wow.'

John and Ted were shaking their heads ruefully, while Linda was already handing out paper plates and warning Len to go easy on the cheese: '…because I don't want you being sick on the bed again like last year.'

'Even health food looks good here, doesn't?' Emma said. 'Wait for it. Here comes Ellie with the speech.'

Ellie climbed up on to a chair and called for quiet. 'Thank you so much for your help, everyone,' she said. 'Now, as is tradition, we will enjoy our last healthy meal before Christmas!'

Everyone cheered. Maggie, still a little full from breakfast, helped herself to a moderate portion of salad, only to have Emma slap a forkful of cured meats on her plate.

'Come on, eat up,' she said. 'Waif like you will disappear if you're not careful.'

Maggie patted her stomach. 'I've put on about fifteen pounds and I've only been here three days.'

'Ah, you'll burn it off. It's all trekking and dancing from Christmas until New Year.'

'I'm leaving on the twenty-seventh.'

'All first-timers say that. Here's Ellie. You can tell her you're staying on.'

'I haven't cleared it with my boss!'

'Never heard of Christmas flu? It's a shocking ailment that always seems to strike at this time of year.'

Ellie was greeting people as she moved through the crowd. When she reached where Maggie stood with Emma and Linda she paused and looked Maggie up and down.

'Wow, you really dressed for eating,' she said. 'You could fit two of you in those jeans. They look kind of familiar … did you get them in Inverness?'

Maggie grimaced. 'They're on loan,' she said. 'From, um, Henry.'

'Oh.' Ellie blinked. '*Oh.*'

'It's not like that. I was up at the reindeer farm and I got a bit dirty—I mean, not dirty, but like with mud—'

Elle patted her on the arm. 'It's all right with me, dear. It's very all right with me.'

'Maggie was hoping to extend her stay through New Year,' Emma said.

'No, I—'

Ellie smiled. 'It's all right; it's already been confirmed.'

'What? By who?'

'Your friend Renee called me earlier. She told me she felt you needed longer to recover from your heartbreak.'

'My—oh, God.'

'She insisted that you be given extra comfort food and booze.'

'I'm going to—' Maggie clenched her fists and stamped her good foot on the ground.

Ellie laughed. 'You have the best best friend in the world.'

Maggie grinned. 'I do, don't I? I wish she was here. She'd love it. She just has her work.'

Ellie winked. 'Well, you'd better not disappoint her, then.'

'I'll try not to.'

As Ellie wandered off, Emma dumped another forkful of meat on Maggie's plate. 'That's settled then, isn't it? And since you're sticking around, no reason to worry about your weight. Come on, eat up.'

32

THE CHRISTMAS MESSAGE

MAGGIE FELT LIKE SHE'D BARELY FINISHED LUNCH when she was being herded back out into the village square for the unveiling of the giant Christmas pudding. The clouds had parted completely now, revealing a glittering blue sky and a cold winter's sun which left the blanket of snow lying over the village like a shiny carpet. The chill had returned, and even though people could see her clearly now the snow was gone, Maggie was grateful for Henry's thick sweater.

A microphone had now been set up on the stage, and a stack of wooden pallets dragged to the middle of the square. Gail, Sally, and a couple of others loitered with bags of paper cups and plastic spoons while Ellie climbed onto the stage and adjusted the mike before giving it a little tap.

'Hello, everyone. Thanks for coming. Are you all ready? It's now time for one of our grandest events here in Hollydell: the great Christmas pudding unveiling. I'm afraid the pudding is a little shy this year, so we'll need you all to clap and cheer to draw it out.'

'If they've pulled the man-in-a-suit trick I'll be mortified,' Emma whispered to Maggie as the crowd began to cheer. 'I've been putting all my food on your plate.'

A door opened in the screen beside the stage, and Phillip appeared, accompanied by Andrew and Jim. All three wore Christmas hats with jingling bells as they struggled with a huge wooden plate loaded with the biggest Christmas pudding Maggie had ever seen. It was the size of the mounds of earth her father had often made around their vegetable garden each spring when he insisted on "changing the soil."

'Wow, I didn't know you could make them that big,' she muttered.

'I think it takes a bit of extra mixing,' Emma said. 'Like with a spade or something.'

'It's enormous.'

'Last year's topped the scales at eighty kilos,' Emma said. 'But that was a runt compared to this.'

The three men lugged the monster to the pile of trestles and set it down. The wood groaned under the weight. Phillip rubbed his back, while Jim gave his arms a quick windmill and Andrew leaned on his knees, puffing out his cheeks. The pudding glistened in the sunlight. It looked traditional, a shiny mixture of mincemeat, fruit and nuts.

'This year's pudding was lovingly created this last January, using a blend of fruit grown in our own greenhouses, nuts harvested in Hollydell's surrounding forest, and fine spices from Waitrose in Inverness. Now, to declare the ceremonial pudding ready to eat, I'd like to invite Jim, our town crier, onto the stage.'

Jim, still rubbing his back, climbed up and took the microphone from Ellie.

'Welcome, one and all,' he said, wincing a little. 'This year, the pudding is our biggest ever. One hundred and fifteen kilograms. And … as those of you who have been here before can testify, you know what has to happen. It all has to go before we can read the inspirational Christmas message written on this year's plate. Every … last … crumb.'

Ellie leaned in and whispered something in his ear.

'The ceremonial pudding will this year be cut by its chief architect and owner of our local delicatessen, Phillip Anderson. And Ellie would like me to point out that one side will be fired with brandy for the drinkers, and one side will be left plain. However, whichever way you lean, there's no excuse for not getting stuck into the clotted cream, which can be found in buckets on the trestle table outside the hotdog stall. If you're worried about your waistline, don't forget, the post-Christmas fat-buster trekking course begins on Boxing Day.'

Several people, including Emma, cheered.

'And also,' Jim said, 'before you dive in, we need to cut off a small chunk for a party who are yet to arrive. No Christmas guest should miss out.'

More clapping and cheers.

'So, finally … Merry Christmas!'

Maggie stared as Jim yodelled his final two words,

drawing them out several syllables longer than usual and bringing the biggest cheer of all.

Phillip produced a double-handled saw. He lifted it over the top of the pudding for Sally to take the other end. Then, lifting one hand, he said, 'Merry Christmas, everyone. May this year's message be an inspiration to you all,' and began to saw.

The pudding spilt like a tree struck by thunder, one rounded top becoming two twin peaks. Phillip produced a bottle of fine Scottish brandy which he poured over one side and then lit to more cheers. Then, stepping back, he allowed the crowd to move in. Smiling people took plates and spoons from Gail, who was handing them out quicker than a casino card shark could deal, while Ellie pushed through the crowd and frantically hacked off a couple of kilograms with a bread knife. She loaded her chunk onto a separate plate and retreated again.

'Come on,' Emma said, nudging Maggie. 'If you're gonna go full calorie, got to go hard, right?'

Maggie grinned. 'Right.'

Just in front of them, Linda shouted, 'Go easy on the cream, Len! Just one dollop per helping!'

Within a couple of minutes, everyone in the assembled crowd was eating Christmas pudding. Maggie made a vague attempt to count the number of people but kept getting lost around eighty. Even with everyone seemingly with a spoon in their hand, however, barely a dent had been made in the pudding.

'It takes a lot more eating than you'd think,' Ted

said, finishing his last mouthful and wiping his mouth with a handkerchief. 'Who's for more?'

Maggie had never eaten anything so sweet and rich in her life. She'd only taken a small piece, but it was sitting heavily on her stomach. With a resigned grin, she followed Ted back toward the pudding, holding out her plate for Phillip to refill.

Second time around, her plate was loaded. She stared in dismay. 'Merry Christmas,' Phillip said with a wink. 'Don't forget the cream. It's right over there. There's no amount of calories that a good hike won't burn off.'

Slowly, the monstrous pudding decreased in size, until at last Phillip scraped away the final crumbs and offered them to Ellie, who had eaten so much she was sitting on the ground. She tried to wave them away, but a grinning Phillip insisted.

'And now it's time to unveil the Christmas message for this year,' Phillip said, as Jim and Gail carried the empty plate up to the stage. 'Everyone, please gather round.'

A group that was now more stomach than human assembled around the stage. Some people were laughing or patting each other on the back, but most were groaning and rubbing their stomachs. Everyone looked stuffed.

Jim and Gail lifted the plate and tilted it forward. Phillip had wiped it down, and now, taking the microphone, he read out the swirl of words emblazoned on its surface.

'And … this year's Christmas message is: "Seize the

day. Don't waste another moment. Today could be your last, so live it as though it is."'

Everyone cheered. Maggie nodded thoughtfully. She looked around for Henry, but he was nowhere about. He had promised to let her help with the reindeer, but perhaps he had gotten busy and forgotten. Maybe she would bump into him later, maybe not.

'Seize the day,' she said.

'What?' Emma said beside her. 'Oh, nice quote, eh? They always roll out something like that. Last year's was "every moment matters", if I remember right. So, how are you going to act on it?'

'I'm going for a little walk,' Maggie said. 'You know, just to burn off the four plates of Christmas pudding I just ate.'

'Would you like some company?'

Maggie shook her head. 'No, I have something I need to do.'

Emma narrowed her eyes. 'Are you sure you're just going for a walk?'

Maggie shook her head. 'No. I'm going to seize the day,' she said.

33

REINDEER

MAGGIE HADN'T BEEN BACK TO COMFORT COTTAGE since the morning, and she found the road lined by big drifts of freshly churned snow left by Andrew's plough. The snowfall which had continued until mid-morning had added a couple more centimetres since, and Maggie's boots left a lonely trail in the snow behind her as she hiked up the hill.

While Andrew had ploughed the road, no one had dug out her path, so she got a few minutes' exercise with a shovel she found in a shed around the side, clearing the path and the verge outside.

With her path lined by neat piles of snow, she went inside and took off her boots. She had planned to change out of the clothes Henry had lent her, but she found herself wanting to keep them on, just to keep the feel and the smell of him close. It was a little obsessive, she knew, but it was Christmas, and she let herself indulge her childlike fantasies, the same way she had tried to convince herself that Santa was a real person even into her mid-teens, and it had got to the point where if she wanted him to eat the mince pies and milk she left for him, she had to sneak downstairs after her parents had gone to bed and take them for herself.

She made a cup of coffee then sat down at the telephone table to call Renee. There was so much she wanted to talk about, and even though she tried to convince herself she didn't need Renee's relentless geeing up, a little pushing wouldn't hurt, just to keep her ship steering in the right direction.

Rather surprisingly, there was no answer. After five rings, Renee's mobile went to voicemail. When Maggie tried again, it cut off entirely, as though Renee had seen the call and ended it.

Maggie frowned. Was something wrong? It was Christmas Eve. Renee would probably be busy, but she always had time to talk to Maggie, and she would want an update on the situation with Henry.

Perhaps it was a deliberate ploy to push Maggie out of her comfort zone. Maggie stared at the phone. She had planned to go on up to Simon's place and look for Henry, but now she was getting cold feet, and not just in the literal sense. What if an afternoon of fixing bolts and waxing runners had tempered the hint of passion Maggie had sensed over breakfast?

'Come on, Renee, pick up,' she grumbled, trying one last time. Again, the dialling tone went straight to voicemail. 'Hi, Renee, this is Maggie. If you get a chance, please give me a call back. Love you.'

She hung up. It was no good. Whatever Renee was

doing, she didn't have time to top up Maggie's fragile confidence. Maggie had to do it for herself.

She had to seize the day.

In the end she did change her clothes, but only because she wasn't comfortable being seen by Simon in his son's shirt and jeans. Picking a pair of trousers and a sweater she hoped were suitably winter-casual-yet-cute, she pulled on her spare jacket on and headed back out.

The sky was still clear as she turned up the road toward Simon's place. Her heart was in her mouth as she walked up the street, conscientiously patting her stomach every few steps to see if the obvious overload of Christmas pudding had tightened up yet. Every miniscule bit of reason told her to stop being so stupid, but the nervous girl inside her wouldn't listen. Henry would reject her. He would tell her he had made a mistake. He would tell her that no one as cultured and world-worthy as he would be interested in a simple shop assistant from Cambridge.

She was halfway there when she saw Henry rounding the corner coming the other way. Maggie's resolve flat-lined, and she ground to a halt, stopping in the middle of the road as she waited for him to arrive.

'Hey,' he said. 'I was wondering where you were. I called Mother down at the village hall, but she told me you'd wandered off somewhere.'

'You were looking for me?'

'Of course.'

'I was, um, just going for a walk,' she said. 'I ate three bowls of pudding.'

'Mother let you get away with just three?'

Maggie shrugged. 'Well, actually it was four, but I didn't want to sound greedy.'

'I rarely got away with less than six,' Henry said. 'That's one reason I didn't go. Takes months to work all that pudding off.'

Maggie slapped a hand over her stomach. 'I feel like a beached whale.'

Henry laughed. 'You look fantastic. Don't worry, we can burn those calories off together.'

How how how how? Maggie's inner voice wailed, picturing a darkened bedroom—or were the curtains open, letting in the light of Christmas morning? What would she say if he asked? What would she—

'There's still a lot of work to do up at Father's place,' Henry said. 'The harnesses weigh a ton until they're properly balanced. The rest of the deer are waiting to meet you, though. You didn't think I'd forget a promise, did you?'

Maggie shook her head, at the same time shaking thoughts of tangled sheets and naked limbs out of her head. 'No, of course not.'

Henry watched her for a few seconds, his eyes studying her face.

Just like, grab him and give him a snog or something, Renee's voice chirped up.

'Be quiet, Renee,' Maggie muttered under her breath.

'Sorry?'

'Um, nothing. So, what's the plan?'

Henry held out a hand. 'Follow me.'

Maggie stared. He had taken off his glove, and,

thanks to the strain of an uphill walk in the snow, she wasn't wearing one either.

Her fingers were shaking as she reached out. There was a moment of uncertainty as their fingers bumped, then his closed around hers. His palm was warm, his fingers strong.

'This way,' he said.

'Uh-huh.' Maggie's heart was thundering so hard her eyes were going blurry. 'I can't see the road,' she muttered.

Henry laughed. 'Did you eat the side with the brandy? Phillip proper pours it on, doesn't he?'

As they walked, they talked about idle nothings. Maggie could barely remember a sentence after it was out of her mouth, and at times she thought she was floating as Henry laughed at her pathetic attempts at jokes, nodded with interest at her inane ramblings, and didn't seem bothered at all when she went on about subjects she barely knew anything about. He watched her carefully, for all the world appearing to like her.

That's because he thinks you're awesome, Renee shouted.

Maggie was almost sad to reach Simon's place.

'Hey, Father,' Henry called. 'I've got someone I'd like you to meet.'

Simon appeared out of the shed. He was holding a wrench and wearing dirty overalls. His white beard bobbed in front of him, and spectacles were pushed over his forehead.

'Oh, we've met. Hey, Maggie.'

'Hello again.'

Simon patted Maggie on the shoulder. 'Thank you

so much for getting Henry out of that river this morning,' he said. 'He was very lucky that you came along.'

'That's all right. It was quite exciting really.'

'And no harm done. That's the end of it. I bet that wasn't the kind of adventure you expected when you decided to visit Hollydell, was it?'

Maggie shook her head. Talking to Simon was strange, as though she were being interviewed. She could almost imagine him patting her on the head and handing her a small gift.

'No, it certainly wasn't,' Maggie said.

'I'm so glad Henry's finally got a new friend,' Simon said. 'All that time sitting around at home … he really needs to get out a bit more.'

'Father, don't,' Henry whined, shooting Maggie a pained glance that made her both laugh and blush.

'His mother and me, we've … well, we'd better get harnessing the deer. It takes a while, and they fidget so much. Do you know much about reindeer, Maggie?'

Maggie shook her head, partly relieved the conversation had changed, and partly disappointed Simon hadn't been even more blatant.

'Not much, I'm afraid.'

'Beautiful creatures,' Simon said. 'Built for the winter. Their hooves actually contract during the winter when the ground is hard, and some species have knees that make a clicking sound so they can hear each other during a blizzard.'

Inside the shed, the sleigh Maggie had seen was covered in a grey sheet again, but a series of wooden harnesses and ropes had been laid out on the snow in front of it. Maggie counted ten.

'They're called reindeer because of their reins, right?' Maggie said.

Simon laughed. 'Actually, their name comes from the old Norse word "hreinn", which means "deer". Although in the USA they're known as caribou, a word that comes from French. I don't remember the exact word, but it translates as "snow-shoveller". I guess it's apt, as where they tend to live, they spend most of their time digging beneath the snow, looking for food.'

Henry was standing nearby, looking awkward, as though his father's knowledge was showing him up. Maggie wanted to laugh at this display of sensitivity, but was worried it would upset Henry. Instead she just gave him a smile.

'We've already herded the deer over from the farm,' Simon said. 'They're in the shed at the back, eating lunch.'

'No Christmas pudding?' Maggie said, then immediately regretted the awkward attempt at a joke.

Both Henry and Simon laughed harder than it deserved. 'No, actually we feed them turnips during the winter,' Simon said. 'They live off moss and lichens when there's not much to eat, but we want them to have plenty of vitamins, keep them strong. Henry, why don't you two bring them around?'

Henry nodded, looking pleased to have been given a task. He waved for Maggie to follow and led her around the main shed to a smaller one at the rear.

'I hope you don't think Father's too boring,' he said. 'He can talk about reindeer all day.'

'It's fascinating,' Maggie said. 'All I know about them is that they have red noses.' At Henry's frown, she said, 'That's a joke.'

'We did have one called Rudolph a few years ago,' Henry said. 'He pulled the sleigh a couple of times as a young buck before his antlers started to shed during the winter, but Father said the kids would get disappointed that he didn't have a red nose, so we quietly changed his name one year to Randolph, and no one noticed. That was when I was a boy, though, and poor old Randolph went off to the great herd in the sky the year before last.'

'What a shame.'

Henry smiled. 'The current lot is all raring to go,' he said. 'You've met George, but let's go and meet the others.'

Maggie had seen some of the reindeer at a distance, but close up she realised that George was a mere child compared to some of the others. Most of them were huge, shaggy beasts with enormous antlers and big, inquisitive eyes. Henry talked about them with real affection as he gave them names like Gallia, Clementine, Mabel, and Catherine. Maggie remembered that all the ones pulling the sleigh would be female, and she found herself feeling an uncanny sense of jealousy.

'I was expecting Donner and Blitzen,' she said, patting one called Juliana on the head as the reindeer tried to nuzzle her.

Henry laughed. 'The names are for us, but we let the people call them what they choose. If Donner and

Blitzen work for you, that's fine. Just don't shout the wrong name when you want to make a turn. They're pretty stubborn beasts.'

One by one, Maggie helped Henry lead the reindeer around to the front and arrange them in their harnesses. The whole process of keeping them still while they were harnessed up, checked, organised, adjusted, and occasionally retrieved after they slipped loose and wandered off, took far longer than Maggie had expected. They were still only halfway through when the sun dropped behind the hills, taking with it the last warmth of day.

Simon, dressed now in a thick woolly hat and an overcoat, came out from the shed and hailed them.

'Maggie, I just got a call from Ellie down at the village hall. She was wondering where you'd got to.'

'Sorry, I don't think I told anyone where I was going.'

'I told her you were safe and sound with us, but she wants you to come back down to the village. There's something she needs you for.'

'Oh?'

'She didn't say what, but she was pretty insistent.' Simon laughed. 'When my wife calls, you'd better answer.'

Maggie felt crestfallen at the thought of leaving Henry, but the phone call had intrigued her.

'Okay, sure.' She turned to Henry. 'Well, I'll see you later, I guess.'

'Can you spare me for a few minutes, Father? It gets dark quickly and the roads will get icy. What with

Maggie hurting her ankle the other day, I think it would be best if I walk her as far as the top of the village.'

Simon winked at Maggie. 'Of course. Just don't get too distracted. I'm getting too old to handle all this on my own.'

Henry nodded. 'I won't be long.'

Maggie said goodbye to Simon, and together, she and Henry headed for the road. Alone again, Maggie felt the awkwardness return, and words deserted her. They had nearly reached the first bend in the road before Henry cleared his throat.

'I, um, heard you were staying until New Year.'

Maggie's cheeks burned despite the cold. 'So did I. My friend booked it for me, apparently. My boss will probably punish me until summer, but I'm glad.'

'I'm glad too.'

'Are you?'

'Yes.'

Maggie nodded. 'That's nice.'

They walked in silence for a while. 'What was this year's Christmas message?' Henry said at last.

'"Seize the day."'

'Oh. It's a good one, I suppose.'

'Yes.'

They walked on a little farther. The awkwardness was killing Maggie. Inside her head, Renee was jumping up and down, screaming at her to do something, but whenever Maggie felt she'd found the perfect sentence and opened her mouth, she found no sound would come out.

At last the lights of the village appeared below them.

They passed a couple of houses and then they were standing at the end of her path.

'I cleared the snow,' Maggie said.

'You've done a great job.'

'Thanks.'

Henry looked as though he wanted to say something, but after a few seconds he just threw a thumb over his shoulder and said, 'I'd better get back. Father will be stressing out. It's a busy night for him.'

He started to turn, but Maggie finally found her voice. 'Henry….'

'Yes?'

'I….' Her mouth had dried up again. '…had a good time.'

'Um, great. See you later.'

He turned and was gone, moving far too quickly, nervously, hurrying along the verge, his hands in his pockets. Maggie waited, but this time he didn't look back. He disappeared around the curve and was gone.

For a few seconds she just stared at the empty road. Then, letting out a sharp cry of frustration, she sat down on the step with her head in her hands.

34

LATECOMERS

'THERE YOU ARE. COME ON, HURRY UP OR WE'LL be late.'

'Late for what?'

Ellie rolled her eyes. 'The train doesn't usually run on Christmas Eve, but we had a special party coming in today so Andrew went to Inverness to pick them up. A few of us have decided to give them a special Hollydell welcome. Plus, it'll get you in the mood for the Christmas Eve extravaganza.' Ellie looked around as though someone else was hiding under a drift of snow.

'Isn't my son with you?'

'He said he had to help Simon.'

Ellie rolled her eyes. 'That boy of mine … honestly.' She put a hand on Maggie's shoulder and steered her toward the road leading down to the station. 'Come on. We're going to sing some carols to greet our new guests. Is your singing voice ready?'

Maggie smiled. 'I have a bit more juice in the tank.'

'Then let's go.'

Under the trees it was dark and the air was chilly, but fairy lights lined the roads, the snow having been shaken off. By the time they reached the small square outside the station, about twenty people had assembled. Gail was handing out song sheets while Sally tried to get them organised. John and Ted were shaking snow off the Christmas tree, Linda was fixing a broken clasp on Len's coat, and Emma was practicing her soprano, much to the frustration of the group standing nearest.

From out in the forest came a blast of the train's horn.

'They're coming,' Ellie said. 'Right, let's do something to warm up. How about *Silent Night?*'

By the time the train rolled into the station, Sally had shunted them into rough groups by vocal range. Maggie was in the alto group, even though she wasn't sure what that meant. Several people were wondering what they ought to sing, when Sally announced the next song would be *Santa Claus is Coming to Town*.

'Just sing it however you like,' she said.

The chatter of excited voices came from through the station doors. Maggie asked Emma who the new guests were, but Emma just shrugged. 'No idea.'

A group of children burst through the doors. Each one wore a Christmas hat, and every one of them looked utterly delighted.

'Three, two, one…!' Sally shouted, and then they burst into a version of the Christmas classic that was only marginally better than it had sounded on karaoke night. Maggie, trying not to laugh at Linda's wild gestures, lost her place on the lyric sheet and squinted at the words in the square's flickering lights.

When she looked up, a petite blonde-haired girl with elfish ears poking out of a Christmas hat, green pixie boots, and a red jacket over a skirt that was criminally short stood by the doors, looking around expectantly.

'Renee!'

'Maggie!'

Maggie broke from the group, aided by what she guessed was supposed to be a helpful shove from Emma. Renee, unsuccessfully trying to herd the children into a group, jumped up and down then rushed forward.

They caught each other in a warm hug.

'You didn't answer your phone!'

'I messaged you, but then I remembered that you smashed your phone to get back at that jerk. Maggie, it's so great to see you. We managed to get a last-minute budget flight from Stansted, and the staff were kind enough to say they'd pick us up.'

Ellie came over. Behind her, led by Sally, the ramshackle choir was hammering out *All I Want for Christmas is You*, with Emma shamelessly trying to ape the vocal histrionics.

'Renee? We spoke on the phone. Thank you for coming.'

Renee looked around at the group of children. 'This place is just … amazing!'

'You've seen nothing yet,' Maggie said. 'Thanks for extending my stay, by the way.'

Renee shrugged. 'Thundercloud bit it totally when I showed up at your shop all coughing and spluttering.

She wouldn't get within five feet of me. I gave her this chocolate cake I bought in Tescos which I said you made for her as a sorry gift. That softened her a bit.'

'You told her I made a cake you got from Tescos?'

Renee shrugged. 'I took it out of the packaging and changed the plate it was on. I put a couple of finger marks in it and put the little ornaments a bit wonky. She'll never know.'

'You're the best.'

Renee grinned. 'Well, kind of. I needed you to help me with the kids a bit. Twenty-five of them to keep a tab on. Should be a delight.'

'We have Christmas pudding and hot chocolate waiting up in the village square,' Ellie said.

Renee nodded. 'Nice. Weigh them down a bit. I nearly lost three of them back in the airport when they wandered off to look at the shops.' She spun around in a circle. 'Wow, I just can't get enough of this place. No wonder they didn't post any photos. It would get swamped.'

'We prefer to cater to a small but enthusiastic crowd,' Ellie said. Then, giving Renee a hug, she said, 'Thank you for coming. I can promise your kids a truly magical Christmas, one they'll never forget.'

As Ellie headed off, Renee leaned close. 'Okay, where's the dish? Henry, wasn't it?'

'He's up at his father's place, harnessing a group of reindeer to a sleigh.'

'Wow! So he's really Santa Claus? That's awesome. You know you could end up being married and having to go out on the sleigh every Christmas Eve.'

Maggie rolled her eyes. 'I think you've watched too many Christmas movies.'

'When am I going to meet him?'

Maggie grimaced. 'Hopefully later on.'

'I hope he's as good-looking as his brother.'

'His brother?'

'The train driver. Oh, he's so cute. I could just eat him up.'

As Andrew came through the doors and tipped his cap to the assembled children, Maggie couldn't help but laugh.

'He doesn't have a chance, does he?'

Renee shook her head. 'Nope.'

35

THE GRAND ARRIVAL

A BAND WAS PLAYING IN THE VILLAGE SQUARE WHEN Maggie arrived, arm in arm with Renee, who would occasionally dart off to retrieve a child about to go exploring into the forest. Maggie was disappointed not to see Henry among them, but Phillip from the delicatessen turned out to be a pretty impressive guitarist, and with Jim yodelling away to a succession of Christmas standards, the large crowd already gathered was having a merry time.

As Ellie and Gail organised hotdogs, burgers, and Christmas pudding for the children, Maggie introduced Renee to her new friends. John and Ted kissed one cheek each, Linda warned her not to let Len give her any eating advice, and Emma greeted her with a large glass of mulled wine, because 'You'll probably need one after dragging that lot all the way up from Cambridge.'

The children and Renee were staying in a dormitory a short walk from the village square. Andrew delivered their luggage on the back of the snow-plough, and Ellie took the children on a quick tour of the village, leaving Renee to relax for a while.

'So, when's he going to show?' Renee said. 'I can't wait to have a look at him.'

Maggie sighed. 'I don't know what's going on, Ren,' she said. 'I mean, it's Christmas Eve. Yesterday I was effectively dumped. I spent the morning wearing a man's clothes after helping him save a reindeer from a river. He's gorgeous, and kind, and intelligent, and strong, and basically everything else. I'm a school leaver who works in a clothes shop five hundred miles away.'

'You're smiling.'

'What? No, I wasn't.'

'You were. What does your intuition tell you? Does he like you or not?'

'I have no idea.'

'Maggie! Just grab him!'

'I knew you'd say that. It's not quite as easy in practice as it is in theory, though, is it?'

'Ah, you're making things way too complicated. It's Christmas.'

'He said he wasn't interested in a holiday romance.'

'Why does it have to be a holiday romance?'

'Because I live in Cambridge!'

'You rent a pokey flat above a greengrocer.'

'I like my job.'

'But you don't like the Thundercloud, do you?'

'No, but—'

'There's a Next in Inverness. All you have to do is fill out a form.'

'What? How did you—'

'I checked on the internet. Stop putting walls in the way. You remember how we completely lucked out on finding this place? It's fate, Mags. And anyway, if he's too hard to get, I'll have a word with him.'

'You're the best, Ren.'

'What are friends for?'

The music suddenly cut out. Maggie looked around as a hush fell over the crowd.

'What's going on?' Maggie asked Emma, who was standing nearby, drinking a paper cup of something that smelled like wine but had a chocolate flake sticking out.

'You're going to love this. It's time for the big man.'

'What, you mean—'

'Yep.'

Blustering and panting, Ellie ran up to them, a group of grinning kids at her shoulder. 'We had a snowball fight in the park,' she said. 'But we're back. I think they're all here.'

Renee did a quick headcount. 'All good,' she said.

'Great. Make sure they don't go anywhere.'

Ellie ran to the stage and took the microphone. Breathlessly, she said, 'It's Christmas, everyone! I'd like you to welcome the man who makes Christmas Christmas. Saint Nick, Father Christmas, Santa Claus himself!'

There was a great rustling of tiny bells that seemed to come out of the forest. Everyone turned to look up the street at a glow that had appeared through the trees. It was coming closer, moving around the bend in the road, and then it was there, a great, majestic sleigh lit by hundreds of fairy lights and pulled by ten magnificent reindeer. At the reins sat a man in a shining red suit, his white hair glowing under the lights, and in the sleigh behind him was the largest sack Maggie had ever seen.

'No way!' one of the boys shouted. Then they were all whooping and cheering as the sleigh made its way down the road and pulled to a stop in the middle of the village square.

'Who wants to meet Santa Claus?' Ellie called from the stage. 'Make a line, please.'

Gail, Sally, and a couple of others ran through the crowd, pulling all the children forward and organising them into a ragged line. Santa Claus, sitting high up on his sleigh, waved to the crowd as they cheered.

'Is that him?' Renee asked. 'He's a bit old.'

'No! That's, um, Santa Claus. He's not … here.'

But even as she said it, a man jumped down from the back of the sleigh with a smaller bag that bulged with angular items. He opened a door in the sleigh's front and lifted a hand to help Santa climb down.

He was wearing a forest green elf's outfit, complete with pointed boots and a hat.

'Henry,' Maggie said, unable to keep the smile off her face. 'He always appears in the strangest of places.'

'Oh, that's beyond awesome,' Renee said, holding Maggie's arm as she jumped up and down. 'Please, please tell me that's him.'

'That's him.'

'Oh, wow! What a dish! Look at the way his muscles bulge through that … what do they call those things? A habit? A waistcoat? And he's so cute. Oh, you're such a great couple.'

'We're not a couple.'

'You should be. He's adorable, just like his brother.'

As Maggie made a mental note to introduce Renee and Andrew later, Henry looked up, spotted her in the crowd, and smiled.

'He totally just checked you out.'

'No, he didn't, he was looking at, I don't know, Ted or someone.'

'You're such a liar. He's smitten.'

Helped by some crowd marshalling by Gail and Sally, Santa Claus made his way to the stage, his helper elf trailing along behind him with the bag of presents. Jim was keeping a hand on the reins of the front reindeer, occasionally allowing a curious boy to pet one.

Santa sat down on a chair as Ellie came across with a microphone.

'Welcome to our town,' she said. 'I guess it's been a long journey?'

Santa laughed. 'Oh, it's been wondrous,' he said in a deep, bellowing voice. 'I'm back in my favourite place in the world.'

'And we're very happy to have you, as always.'

As Ellie put Santa through a series of questions, then fielded some from the kids—the most amusing of which was 'Do you have frogs in the North Pole?'—Henry squatted nearby, holding the bag, occasionally casting glances out at the audience.

'So, he's a vet, a poet, a musician, a professional chess player, and he makes his own jam?'

'I'm not sure about the jam.'

'And on top of everything, he's an elf, and his dad is Santa Claus.' Renee jumped up and down. 'Oh, you've totally lucked out.'

'And I'm a thirty-something nobody from Cambridge barely making above minimum wage. What could he possibly find interesting about me?'

Renee nudged Maggie in the ribs. 'Oh, you just don't get it, do you? At the end of the day, none of that stuff matters. Okay, maybe the elf part does. We're people, and we go person to person, and if one person matches another person, we're all good. You're a lovely, kind person, and if he's willing to stand on stage dressed as an elf, then he clearly is too. Game on.'

'She's right,' Emma said. 'Although I don't believe anyone needs a man in their life. Bloodsuckers, the lot of them.'

'Everyone needs a man in their life,' John said. 'Especially one willing to dress like that. Ted, I told you we should have got that costume. They have your size in the shop.'

'You can borrow Len's,' Linda said, then laughed uncomfortably loud, making the rest of them wince.

On the stage, Gail was ushering the children forward one by one to have a word with Santa and receive a gift. Sally moved through the crowd, making sure no one was forgotten. Jim patted the reindeer as they waited patiently then called frantically for Phillip to bring a shovel as one of them did its business in the middle of the village square.

At last Santa Claus was done, and the bag of

presents was nearly empty. Ellie thanked him for coming, he wished the crowd a Merry Christmas, and then made his way back to the sleigh, Henry following behind.

Santa climbed up into the front and Henry climbed into the back through a little gate. With a flick of the reins, the reindeer began to move as the crowd parted in front of them.

'Now's your chance,' Renee said.

'What?'

'Look!'

Maggie had been transfixed by the deer and their red-clad figurehead, but as Renee tugged her arm, she saw Henry leaning over the side, looking right at her. He lifted a hand and beckoned her forward.

'Go!'

Maggie didn't have much choice as Renee shoved her from behind. She darted out of the crowd, up to the back of the sleigh, and onto a step in front of the little gate. Henry reached out and pulled her through, then snapped the gate shut behind them.

Everyone was so transfixed by Santa and the reindeer that no one except Renee and Emma seemed to have noticed. Both gave her a thumbs-up as the sleigh glided away.

'Hey,' Henry said, as they slid out of the village square and up the road that led back around to the reindeer farm. 'Thanks for joining me. I hope you like my outfit.'

Maggie laughed. 'It's fetching.'

'You know, you can borrow it any time.'

'I'll remember that.'

They had passed the last of the houses and the forest was sliding past. Over the glow of the lights, it was nearly impossible to see anything beyond the huge sack looming over their heads.

'What's in there?' Maggie asked. 'Did you fill it with wood or something? It certainly looks impressive.'

'It's full of presents.'

'Really? Who for?'

'The others.'

'What others?'

Henry smiled. As he did so, Maggie felt a little tingle as though an electrical current had dusted her fingertips. 'Anyone who needs one.'

They had passed Henry's reindeer farm, and a moment later slid into the tunnel that led to Simon's place. However, as they reached the fork in the road, the sleigh turned off the main road, taking the track led up the hills to what Simon had told Maggie was a lookout point.

'I'm afraid we have to get off in a minute,' Henry said. 'Father has some work to do now.'

As if on cue, the sleigh slid to a stop. From the front came Santa's voice: 'Thank you, lad, and thank you, young lady! Have a great Christmas Eve.'

Henry opened the back gate and helped Maggie down. With the click of the reins, the sleigh moved off up the road, leaving them behind. It disappeared into the trees, then the glow of its lights began to rise as though it were heading up a steep hill. The glow became smaller, slowly decreasing, then was gone.

Henry reached out a hand. 'Shall we take a walk? It's a nice night.'

Maggie was shaking. Unsure of what she had just witnessed, she grabbed Henry's hand a little too hard.

'Ouch!'

The sky had cleared. High above, the Christmas star glittered against the background of other stars.

'Sorry about that. I'm just … nervous.'

'Don't be. It's Christmas. All that's left for us to do is relax.'

The road arched around a bend. Neither said anything, but Maggie's eyes widened as the trees opened out and the road ended in a wide picnic area where several tables poked up out of the snow. From the edge of the picnic area the ground became open and rocky, dropping down a steep slope to the tree line far below.

'Where did he go?'

Henry smiled. 'Where do you think? It's Christmas Eve.'

Maggie felt that same tingle of electricity again. 'You mean … your dad … he's really the real—'

Henry laughed, shaking his head. 'He's not my dad. My dad lives in Inverness. He's the port's harbourmaster. Mum goes back there to live with him during the close season.'

'But you call him "Father"…?'

'Well, "Father Christmas" is a bit of mouthful, when you have to repeat it all year long. There's no close season when you're looking after the reindeer.'

'But everyone else calls him Simon.'

'I think he prefers it. He's quite a reclusive fellow

really, and while it's an open secret here in Hollydell, he wouldn't appreciate people showing up to take photographs in the middle of July.'

Maggie was still dumbfounded. 'I don't know what to say. Did I just see what I thought I just saw?'

Henry laughed. 'You saw what you wanted to see. I think that's about the whole of it. Hollydell is a place where people get to believe in things they might never have believed before. That's the magic of the place. Now, just relax and enjoy the view.'

As Maggie's eyes adjusted, a bright moon and a field of stars illuminated a snow-covered landscape of hills, forests and lakes. She was no longer in Scotland, she was somewhere else, somewhere magical where anything could happen.

'Merry Christmas,' Henry said. 'I got you something.'

Maggie realised for the first time that he had brought the smaller sack, and now pulled a small present from inside.

'What is it?'

'You can open it now if you like.'

Maggie carefully tore the paper, and pulled out a little crocheted handmade hat with a reindeer design on the front.

Maggie turned it over in her hands. 'Oh. I, um, don't know what to say. Did you make it yourself?'

Henry coughed. 'No, I certainly didn't. I bought it from the market.' He grinned. 'It was the only thing I could find that was almost as embarrassing as wearing an elf costume.'

'I think you look fetching.'

'You're too kind. Come on, why don't you try your new hat on?'

Maggie laughed as Henry helped her. It didn't even fit properly, having been made to fit a child's head.

'There,' he said with a wide grin. 'You look shocking. I don't feel so bad now.'

They sat in silence for a while, looking out at the view. Maggie wanted to speak, but she was afraid that anything she said might spoil the moment. Plus, she'd done all the running about. It was time to find out if Henry really liked her.

At last he said, 'I'm glad your boyfriend dumped you.'

'Excuse me?'

'And if he hadn't, I might have tried to steal you anyway.'

Maggie's throat felt dry. 'Steal me?'

'That first time I saw you—when I nearly ran you over with the sleigh—I saw you standing there and I thought you looked absolutely lovely. I lost my grip on the reins, and I nearly ran you down. I'm sorry about that. I mean, that would have been a complete disaster, particularly as George was a little more jumpy than I'm used to.'

'I'm glad you didn't run me down, but I'm also glad you noticed me.'

'It was hard not to. You looked like an angel standing there in the snow. I'd never seen anything so lovely in all my life.'

Maggie laughed. 'Now that's just a line.'

Henry shook his head. 'I don't do lines. I'm about as boring as they come. I farm, I do my introverted things. I enjoy life, but I don't care for bombast or drama. I don't care about money or status. I'm just me, Henry, sitting beside you, Maggie, and being happy that I'm here.'

Maggie lifted a hand to wipe away a tear. 'Thank you. So, you, um....'

'Like you? I hope that's what you were going to say.'

'Yes.'

'Yes.'

'Yes?'

Henry laughed. 'I think you're wonderful. But ... I don't do holiday romances.'

Maggie looked down. 'You said before. I understand.'

Henry's hand closed over hers. 'And as I told you, it's the holiday part I don't like. I mean, it can be part of it and all that. You know, there's a Next in Inverness.'

Maggie laughed. 'And all I have to do is fill out a form?'

'You checked it out too?'

'Renee told me. I'm sure I could handle a change of scenery.'

'But if you didn't Cambridge isn't that far, and we get pretty decent Wi-Fi once the snow's gone. Plus, I spend a lot of the year looking for things to do. Father is around to look after the reindeer once he's done with Christmas, so I travel a lot. There's absolutely no way we can't see each other if we want to.'

'I'd like that.'

Henry reached up and brushed a lock of hair behind her ear. She shivered at his touch. 'The hat's a bit small, I'm afraid.'

'It keeps slipping up.' Maggie grinned. 'But thanks anyway. I'm afraid I didn't get you a present.'

Henry met her gaze. She looked into his eyes as he leaned forward and gave her a light kiss on the lips.

'That will do very nicely,' he said, stroking her cheek.

'Um, I'm a bit cold,' Maggie said, her heart thundering so hard it made her voice tremble. 'I didn't really feel anything. Perhaps you could try again?'

Henry smiled. 'Sure.'

As he leaned in to kiss her again, Maggie took a deep breath, and her heart seemed to fill to bursting with laughter and music and the magic of Christmas as, somewhere far away, bells began to chime, and the voices of a choir began to sing.

'Merry Christmas, Maggie,' Henry said, holding her close.

'Merry Christmas, Henry,' she answered, loving the way his name on her tongue felt natural, as though it belonged there.

And they lived happily ever after...

...the End.

ABOUT THE AUTHOR

CP Ward is a pen name of Chris Ward, the author of the dystopian *Tube Riders* series, the horror/science fiction *Tales of Crow* series, and the *Endinfinium* YA fantasy series, as well as numerous other well-received stand alone novels.

Chris has always wanted to write a Christmas book. This is his first attempt.

There might be more …

Chris would love to hear from you:
www.amillionmilesfromanywhere.net
chrisward@amillionmilesfromanywhere.net

Made in the USA
Las Vegas, NV
20 November 2021

34926147R00156